**"We need to talk. We're not—don't do this, Jack."**

"Seems to me that you're doing it, too, sweetheart."

"I'm trying not to. I don't want to," she said while he stroked his hands down her back and kept up a constant rain of those sweet, hungry kisses.

"Why?"

"Because this isn't enough," she said. "This doesn't make up—it can't make up—for the places that are all wrong."

"It can. We have to work on it, not let it go. When it's this strong, Carmen, you just have to take it on faith and—"

"No. No. Stop." Shakily, she pushed him away and walked out of the house toward his car, parked in the street.

"You still want to eat?" He followed her, sounding angry and at sea.

"I'm hungry," she snapped at him, because it was either *I'm hungry* or *I'm pregnant,* and she didn't want to give him her news that way.

Dear Reader,

I'm a cat person. More specifically, a tuxedo cat person, so you won't be surprised to find that there's a very cute tuxedo kitten in this book. I'd actually written this scene without any recent experience of choosing kittens, but just a few weeks after I wrote it, our much loved ten-year-old black-and-white cat, Gus, died, and my children decided that what we most needed to cheer us up was a new black-and-white kitten…or even better, two.

Sometimes, life does imitate fiction! We went off to the animal shelter and there were the most gorgeous black-and-white boy kittens—twin brothers, seven weeks old, with snowy white tuxedo fronts, glossy black backs. We claimed them instantly.

That night, we all sat around trying to think of the right names, and somehow, without my influence and without the kids' even knowing the names of the characters in this book, our twin kittens ended up with the names Jack and Davey, just like my hero. Although we will never forget our beloved Gus, I cannot tell you how much fun we are having with these two.

I hope you enjoy the story of Carmen, Jack, Ryan… and a kitten named Tux.

*Lilian Darcy*

# A MOTHER
# IN THE MAKING

## LILIAN DARCY

**SPECIAL EDITION**

Published by Silhouette Books

**America's Publisher of Contemporary Romance**

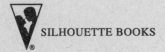 SILHOUETTE BOOKS

ISBN-13: 978-0-373-24880-3
ISBN-10:    0-373-24880-6

A MOTHER IN THE MAKING

Visit Silhouette Books at www.eHarlequin.com

Printed in U.S.A.

**Books by Lilian Darcy**

Silhouette Special Edition

*Balancing Act* #1552
*Their Baby Miracle* #1672
*The Father Factor* #1696
†*The Runaway and the Cattleman* #1762
†*Princess in Disguise* #1766
†*Outback Baby* #1774
*The Couple Most Likely To* #1801
*A Mother in the Making* #1880

Silhouette Romance

*The Baby Bond* #1390
*Her Sister's Child* #1449
*Raising Baby Jane* #1478
*Cinderella After Midnight* #1542
*Saving Cinderella* #1555
*Finding Her Prince* #1567
*Pregnant and Protected* #1603
*For the Taking* #1620
*The Boss's Baby Surprise* #1729
*The Millionaire's Cinderella Wife* #1772
*Sister Swap* #1816

†Wanted: Outback Wives
*The Cinderella Conspiracy

## LILIAN DARCY

has written more than seventy-five books for the Silhouette Romance, Special Edition and Harlequin Medical Romance (Prescription Romance) lines. Happily married, with four active children and two very rambunctious kittens, she enjoys keeping busy and could probably fill several more lifetimes with the things she likes to do—including cooking, gardening, quilting, drawing and traveling. She currently lives in Australia but travels to the United States as often as possible to visit family. Lilian loves to hear from readers. You can write to her at: P.O. Box 532 Jamison PO, Macquarie ACT 2614, Australia, or e-mail her at: lilian@liliandarcy.com.

# Chapter One

Jack heard his cell phone start up when he was partway through the slow, careful process of getting dressed. It was sitting downstairs on the coffee table where he'd left it the night before. Shirtless, barefoot and cursing, he took the stairs too fast, swung around the banister post on the landing halfway down and bumped his shoulder into the opposite wall, which meant that the half-healed wound in his left side was screaming at him by the time he picked up the phone.

T-shirt balled in his free hand and lopsided with pain, he heard Terri's voice. He'd been expecting her call. Had thought about it when he'd lain awake in the night, unable to get back to sleep.

"Sorry, did I get you out of bed?" she cooed at him,

and he caught the veiled put-down like a pro baseball player catching a kid's practice throw.

Yeah, Terri, okay, I get it, you think I'm lazy. It was seven-thirty on a New Jersey Monday morning. Terri's *new* husband, Jay, arose at six every day, went to the gym for an hour, ate a power breakfast and still managed to make a couple of billion dollars by lunch.

"Out of the shower," he told her, after a silence that lasted a fraction too long. His side was still burning and he couldn't be bothered attempting to change what his ex-wife thought of him.

What she thought of him had become pretty clear during the process of their divorce.

The only thing that mattered in their relationship anymore was Ryan, and he mattered down to the marrow of Jack's bones. Ryan came first.

He took some cautious breaths and paced up and down the splintered old hardwood floor, willing the pain to ebb. What had he done in there? Ripped open his stitches? Did the agony show in his voice?

Terri knew that he'd just come out of the hospital, but he'd played the whole thing down when he'd told her what had happened. She no longer considered straight-talking cops to be heroes. Wall Street pirates with fat bank accounts and a polished line in doublespeak were the real he-men, as far as she was concerned.

She hadn't been like this when they were first married at age twenty, fourteen years ago. He'd never seen this side of her back then, when they were so young. Deciding that she didn't love him anymore seemed to have given her the license to fight as dirty as she could, and it set his teeth on edge.

"Did you and Jay have your meeting?" he asked.

"Family council," Terri corrected quickly, as if the distinction was important.

Jack thought it was typical of Jay Kruger that he ran his new family the same way he ran his corporate take-overs, complete with meetings and agendas and power plays, but Terri didn't want to see things this way.

He waited. He wasn't going to dutifully echo the words *family council* just to ease her conscience. Nor was he going to let on how emotional he felt about the possible outcome.

"Yes, we had it…" she said, letting her sentence trail off enticingly.

Jack clenched his jaw. He knew this routine. She wanted him to wait and beg. It was like those pointless thirty-second pauses on reality TV shows before they announced the winner or loser's name. Did his ex really think he didn't see the emotional manipulation?

"Cut to the chase, Terri," he growled at her.

"The chase? I'm not sure that I like what you're implying, Jack. This is not a game."

"I know it's not."

"These are incredibly serious issues."

"I know they're serious issues. Tell me what you and Jay decided."

"See, and I hate to hear you sounding so aggressive. It makes me wonder if I've made the right decision after all…"

His heart leaped. *The right decision.* Did she mean…? "Please tell me straight, and don't keep me dangling." There. She had him begging, the way she wanted. "What decision have you made?"

"I'm getting to that." Her voice pointedly soothed his impatience. "But you need to know the process we went through first. This was not decided lightly, Jack." She gave him several minutes on the nonlightness of the process, her feelings, her priorities, and yet another rehash of how she'd never wanted to hurt him, then finished, "And we feel that the most important issue in all of this, Jack, in *all* of this," she repeated, in case he thought she meant only forty-three percent of it, "has to be Ryan's well-being."

She spoke as if generously sharing a profound new insight. In reality, Jack himself had been making the same point to her for almost three years, as clear and direct as he could, and was never heard. He'd dealt with stalling and manipulation and outright lies. Only six months ago had he resorted to the threat of going to court. "We feel it's not in his best interests to drag him through a court proceeding," she went on.

Noooo, he thought sourly. Really? Not in Ryan's best interests? How perceptive and profound! He never would have thought to consider the issue of Ryan's well-being!

From somewhere nearby there came the sound of a car door slamming, followed by metallic clunkings, and Jack struggled to hear his ex's voice. "…and Jay also wants to pay tribute to your desire to remain involved in Ryan's life."

*Pay tribute to his desire to remain involved?* Was she reading from a script?

"Okay…" Jack said cautiously. The pain in his left side still throbbed, although it had begun to ease. He waited for the other shoe to drop.

"So we've decided to give you what you want," Terri said, and despite that little teaser from her about "the right decision" a couple of minutes ago, he almost didn't believe what he was hearing.

Give him what he wanted?

Just like that?

There had to be a catch!

"Ryan can spend every second weekend with you," she announced. "Friday afternoon through Sunday evening, and three midweek nights, Monday through Wednesday, of every second week."

Okay, so there *was* a catch. Five nights out of fourteen, split into two separate packages, when Jack had wanted seven nights in a row. Ryan didn't need an extra session of packing pajamas and homework and going back and forth.

Still it was so much better than he'd expected.

So much better—enough that he wouldn't push for the seven consecutive nights.

Real, genuine day-to-day time with his nine-year-old son, and no battles to fight along the way. They could start the new arrangement immediately. He had seriously thought that Terri would hold firm on the current grudging one weekend in four unless he took her to court, and he'd been so torn about what was best for

Ryan. He'd tried so hard not to let things get too ugly between himself and Terri, for their son's sake.

Ah, hell…hell…

This was really, really good.

On top of the pain in his side and last night's sleeplessness and bad dreams, the news had him battling his emotions, desperately trying to keep them at bay. He felt his throat tighten, felt the physical wash of relief that made his legs go weak. His eyes began to sting.

He was not going to give in to this! The police counselor kept telling him he was bottling things up, that something would have to give, and that it wouldn't be pretty. She was probably right, but he was *not* going to pop the cork on that bottle now, in front of his ex on the phone.

With the effort of keeping himself in check, he tightened his stomach muscles, and the pain gave another sharp rip at his guts.

"That's good, Terri, that's great," he managed, heading for the kitchen.

Water.

He just needed a glass of water, to loosen up this lump in his throat.

In that direction, he heard a door open, and a clatter.

"But we'll need to work out the exact details…" His ex-wife's tone gave out a warning, like a parent saying, You have to do your homework first.

"Of course." The emotion pushed harder into his chest, and the pain knifed his side. What had he done to himself, coming down those stairs? The doctor had said he was very happy with the way the injury had been healing since the surgery.

"I'll pick him up from school Thursdays because he has violin," Terri was saying.

"I can take him to violin," Jack managed to answer.

"Well, no, because I need to take notes from his teacher on his practice schedule," she explained, as if such a task was quite beyond Jack's abilities.

"Let's talk later, okay?" he said, through teeth clenched from the pain in his side.

"I guess you need to get dressed…"

"Something like that." He disconnected the call and rounded the corner into the kitchen, intending to lean over the sink and just pant and gasp and swear and groan for a while…maybe let the cork out of that bottle…as soon as he'd safely put down the phone. But there was a strange woman standing there with a dilapidated toolbox open on his equally dilapidated kitchen table, and the sight of each other brought both of them up short.

She dropped something back in the toolbox with a metallic clatter, gave a loud, startled squeak and clamped a fist over her heart. "Oh. Didn't hear you!"

Jack gulped back the jagged rock in his throat, dropped the phone onto the kitchen bench and said, "Uh, hi."

Why was there a woman in his kitchen? She had goose bumps on her bare arms and an aura of energy in every limb, and he was confused.

This should be Cormack O'Brien, here to begin work on the kitchen and bathroom remodeling, not this curvy little thing, underdressed for early April in a red cotton

T-shirt and blue denim shorts. She had dangling red earrings that swung back and forth when she moved her head, dark curly hair, brown eyes and tanned skin. She also had an alarmed look getting stronger on her face, and he did not want her here to witness…to witness…

With a heroic effort, he tightened every muscle in his body, shook out his T-shirt ready to put it on, and managed to look…just…as if he was okay.

"You're Jack," Carmen said, taking a large step backward, for safety's sake, her heart beating a little too fast as she looked at the new arrival in the kitchen.

She really, really hoped this man was Jack, shirtless owner of the house, because she wasn't convinced she could tackle him to the ground and put a knee in his back if he was an unwanted intruder. He was tall and strong, and with that bare chest, knotted arm muscles and a crumpled garment dangling from a tight fist, he looked wound up and ready to snap.

"I'm Carmen O'Brien, Cormack's sister," she continued quickly. "The other *C* in C & C Renovations. Cormack is sick and can't work today."

Although she was the one making explanations, Jack Davey looked like the one who thought he didn't belong. "Right," he said. "Right."

"And you're Jack." She managed to avoid making it a question.

"Yes, that's right." He lowered the T-shirt or rag or whatever it was. He was only half-dressed. His feet were bare, and the snap on his ancient jeans was undone.

His dark hair was rumpled and he hadn't shaved in a couple of days. He had cool gray eyes with little crinkles at the corners that she wanted to trust. The crinkles had to say something good about his smile. But he looked so far from smiling right at this moment, he scared her.

Ah. Okay.

With the T-shirt out of the way, she saw the red slash of a barely healed wound slicing across his tanned rib cage, which maybe explained the scary vibes. She wondered what on earth he'd done to himself. Heart surgery? Was that why he looked so serious and struggling and grim?

"I'm sorry about this," he said through a tight jaw. She saw his throat work and his body spasmed. "Side's hurting a bit."

"Oh, of course, it looks nasty."

"I'm sorry," he said again.

"No, no, it's fine. I'm not who you were expecting. I mean, I guess we startled each other." She hadn't been expecting a half-naked, freshly scarred, well-built, thirtysomething man who looked like a bomb about to go off, here to greet her this morning.

"You need to get to work. I'll, uh…"

"No rush. Although it would help me to warm up a bit." She tried a grin as she rubbed the goose bumps on her arms. "I'm dressed for working hard in the middle of the day, not standing around doing nothing early in the morning."

He nodded vaguely, and looked past her, toward the sink. What was wrong with him?

"Um, are you okay?" she tried.

"Fine. I'm fine."

It was such a lie, he could barely get the words out, poor guy. His face was so tight, and his gray eyes were like slits, he'd narrowed them so much. She gentled her voice and told him, "No, you're not."

And then it happened. His stomach began to heave. He pressed the shirt to his face. His shoulders shook. Sounds broke from his mouth.

He was crying.

Crying, with great, deep, scratchy, painful and achingly poignant sounds, and fifteen years of family grief and struggle had taught Carmen an instinctive response that came without her even thinking about it. She stepped close to him, took a hold of his big, warm body and let him sob his heart out in her arms.

## Chapter Two

Carmen didn't know how long they stood this way.

She had to stretch onto her toes to reach Jack Davey properly, even though he was already bent and crooked. The awkward posture must come from protecting that wound on his side. She was careful not to hold him too close because she could tell he was in pain. He laid his head on her shoulder and she cradled it the way she used to do when the sobbing body in her arms belonged to her dad, her sister Melanie or her brother Joe.

Just last night she'd held her other sister like this— eighteen-year-old Kate, after Kate had stumbled in at midnight, and Carmen had yelled at her because she was drunk, and Kate had yelled back, then burst into maudlin tears.

Carmen had run her hands across Kate's wildly streaked hair and soothed her with little sounds and finally told her, "You have to get a grip, honey, you can't let yourself get this messed up. What's wrong?"

Kate had had no answers, and the tears had given way to petulant teen anger. "You have no clue, Carmen! You treat me like a child! How come you can't just leave me alone?" Then she'd half stormed, half lurched off to the bathroom to hang over the sink and lose whatever cocktail of fast food and alcohol was sloshing around in her stomach.

Was there anything else in the cocktail besides alcohol?

Anything stronger?

Carmen was incredibly worried about her and had no idea what to do.

And now she had a stranger crying on her shoulder, and didn't know what to do about that, either. Especially when she discovered that thinking about Kate had made her run her hands across Jack Davey's hair in just the same soothing, helpless way, while she whispered, "It's okay, it's okay, just let it all out."

Oh, Lord, had he noticed what she was doing?

She stilled the movement cautiously, not wanting just to rip her hand away. Resting on his dark head, her fingers found clean springiness and released the damp scent of his musky, nutty shampoo into the air. His body's shaking began to ebb. She lifted her hand and patted his back in a rhythm of rough, awkward beats, finding pads of solid, well-worked muscle. He had the hardest, strongest body she'd ever felt. How could such a body possibly feel so vulnerable in her arms? What was wrong?

"I'm sorry." His voice was like gravel. Or metal, rusted by his tears. "I am so…" he took a shuddery breath "…sorry about this."

"It's fine." She pulled away. "I—I didn't know if—"

"It's okay." He balled the shirt in front of his chest, a defensive maneuver that successfully put some space between them.

Carmen felt a little dizzy for a moment, and the air around her body was too cool again now that his body heat had gone. So strange. Every cell in her body seemed aware of how strong he'd been, and yet she was the one giving comfort. As she'd known for a long time, there was more than one kind of strength in a human being.

While she watched, still helpless as to what she should say or do next, he brought the garment to his face and wiped, as if it was a towel. He pulled it over his head, pushed his arms through the sleeves, looked down at the wet patch on the fabric made by his tears, and pulled it off again. "I'll have to change," he muttered.

"Do you want to…talk, or something?" she offered. "You shouldn't just—"

"I'm okay."

"You're not."

"Well, I'm embarrassed. But I know what this is about."

"Maybe you should tell me. Please don't be embarrassed."

"Yeah, right!" he drawled. "This isn't remotely embarrassing, sobbing on my kitchen contractor's shoulder."

"Well… But no, I mean, you're a human being. We all—"

"Yeah, okay. I mean, the counselor said it would happen. That something like this would happen at some point. I'm sorry you were the one who got hit with it." He massaged the heel of his big hand against his ribs, parallel to the fresh surgical scar. "I just got shot a couple of weeks ago, that's all."

*"Shot?"* she echoed on a gasp, shocked not just at the fact of it, but the way he said it, almost apologetically.

"Line of duty." He'd seen her reaction. "I'm a cop."

"What, so you're…used to it or something?" She was still shocked, line of duty or not.

"I meant, don't go thinking I'm in the middle of a gang war, or I've just come back from a war zone. It's just…it's a risk, in my profession. It was bad luck. And it hurts. They've given me some time off, and I'm taking a backlog of vacation days, too."

"I should think so!"

"But it all got pretty messed up in there—the bullet through my ribs, I mean—so I had surgeons poking around, fixing it up, stitching everything. I strained it, or something, coming down the stairs too fast a minute ago…to catch the phone. It's feeling a little better now."

"That's something. Still, though…"

"But then I got the phone call from—" He stopped. "Yeah. She—the counselor—said I was bottling things up. My emotions. And it might come spilling out for no reason. She said I'd have some really strange reactions, maybe for weeks or even months." He rubbed his side again.

"Is it still hurting bad?" Carmen asked. "Looks to me like it is. Don't you need a doctor?" It seemed easier for both of them to focus on the physical damage, not the emotional, after what had just happened. "You're still not standing straight." He had one big, muscular shoulder lifted forward, and bent over from the waist.

"I'm fine. It looks worse than it is. Or that's what they keep telling me." He gave a sudden grin that dropped from his eyes and mouth far too soon. Carmen wanted it back. It changed his whole face. The man should grin all the time. But he was frowning when he repeated, "I'm fine." Once more he wiped the hem of his shirt across his face.

She nodded. "Mmm. Really?" He didn't look fine. He looked embarrassed, distressed and in serious pain. "Can I get you…?" She waved vaguely, at a loss.

"Glass of water would be good." He nodded toward the faucet and the sink, both of which would be completely gone from here by the end of the day, with the help of C & C's trainee, Rob, and some good tools. Jack looked down at the shirt. "I'd better, uh…"

Without finishing the sentence, he disappeared back the way he'd come. Carmen poured his water, feeling that it was nowhere near enough as a gesture of comfort and support.

Oh, glory!
Jack sank onto the edge of his bed and wiped his

hands down his face. If he just could have drunk the water and been on his own for a minute, he would have been fine, but to be faced by a pair of concerned brown eyes, hands that visibly itched to give a comforting caress and a soothing feminine voice asking that classic, caring question, "Are you okay?"

That was what had broken him. That little question. And then when she'd pushed, after he'd said he was fine. "No, you're not…" Her voice was a honey trap, sweet and clear and straightforward.

He'd never felt so awkward and embarrassed in his life. Sobbing on her shoulder like a kid who'd grazed his knees. He could still feel the way her body had pressed against him. Carefully, because of his wound. Softly, because she had too many curves to be anything but soft—two full breasts and a slightly rounded stomach that she probably thought was too fat. Generously, because it was incredibly generous of her to give him that comfort when they'd only just met and she had no clue what was wrong.

If he hadn't been in floods of tears, he would probably have been aroused. Oh, yeah, he could still smell her on his skin! He lifted a forearm to his nose. Yes. A wholesome, intriguingly different sort of smell, like oatmeal and fresh wood shavings and peach.

"Get a grip, Officer Davey!" he muttered out loud.

He stood up and began to pace and breathe, then wondered if she'd be able to hear him going back and forth like a caged beast. She already thought he was a little scary, with his raw wound and hair-trigger emotions. He couldn't stay here like this when he'd only come up to change his shirt. She deserved some further explanation as to why he was so messed up, even if a heart-to-heart was the last thing he felt like.

He rummaged in a drawer for another old T-shirt suitable for painting in, but his damned eyes were still stinging and what the hell were all his old shirts doing way in the back of the drawer, anyhow, when usually they were the only ones he could find when he looked for a new one?

He let out a string of curse words—which never helped as much as he expected, he'd noticed—dived into the shirt and braced himself for going back down the stairs.

Carmen heard Jack's footsteps overhead, making the old floorboards creak. He returned after a couple of minutes, wearing a fresh T-shirt.

Old, but fresh.

Very old, smelling of lemon detergent.

She could see the contours of his muscles clearly through the thin cotton fabric. Around his thick biceps, the edges of the shirt were frayed. Despite his wounded chest, he was dressed for hard work, and she had an instinct that he needed it. He was the kind of man who hammered out his pain far more often than he cried over it.

She handed him the water. He still looked emotional, like he was struggling, and she blurted out, "I'm sorry, if you've had bad news, or if you need more time, or an appointment with the police counselor you mentioned. If this isn't a good day to start, I can wait until Cormack is better. He just has the flu."

"I had a phone call. Would have been okay without that."

"You mean you would have bottled up your emotions a little longer?"

"Yeah."

"It's a strategy, I guess," she murmured, and waited.

She didn't want to push him on this, but maybe it would be better if he spilled a little more. Better for both of them. She hated the idea of everything hanging in the air, since it was obvious he planned to work on the house today, also.

They would be alone together for hours.

"It wasn't bad news, it was good news, when my ex called just now." He dropped into a kitchen chair and rubbed his wounded side again, then said abruptly, "Might as well tell you so you know, because he'll probably be around when you're here. I'm getting part-time custody of my son, Ryan, without having to go to court over it, after six months of battles. I wasn't expecting it. I'm really happy."

"Yeah, really happy, and that's why you were crying," Carmen drawled, before giving herself a chance to rethink the words. Some people considered her too blunt, but she had no time—literally no time, on a busy day—for playing games.

"You can cry when you're happy, you know," he retorted with a little spirit, "even when you're a guy." He paused for a moment and took several gulps of water, before more words came spilling out. "See, this whole shooting thing… It was a woman, only in her twenties.

She shot me. She was crazy on ice—crystal meth—completely off her face. Don't ever touch that stuff, it's a terrible drug."

"I wouldn't," Carmen said, but she was thinking of Kate.

Kate wouldn't be that stupid, would she? As usual, she felt like a parent instead of an older sister, angry and worried and helpless about what to do with a rebellious teen.

"Then my partner shot her and she died," Jack Davey said.

"Oh, no…"

"He had no choice. There was no other way to get her under control and stop her shooting more. He wasn't aiming to kill, but the light was bad, and she was moving crazy all over the place. It was… People think it's all in a day's work for a cop, shooting and killing, but it's not."

"I'm sure it isn't!" She couldn't begin to imagine.

"No matter what the situation and how much you had no choice, it's still something you live with for the rest of your life. The woman had a kid."

"Oh, no…"

"Maybe it's a blessing. The kid's with her aunt and uncle now, and I was told they're decent people, so maybe she'll have a better life now that her mother is gone. But still."

"When did it happen?"

"Ten days ago."

"Ten days!" No wonder he was raw, physically and emotionally.

"Sheesh, listen to me!" he said. "I'm sorry. You signed on for my kitchen not my therapy."

"It's okay."

"Like the counselor said. We've both been told we'll have some strange responses to things for a while, my partner and I." He paused for a big, slow breath. "Including babbling to strangers." The corner of his mouth twitched wryly.

Carmen could only nod. "It sounds—"

Like a nightmare.

He cut her off. "Yeah. It was."

She got his don't-want-to-talk-about-it-anymore message loud and clear. "Seriously, I can start tomorrow."

He thought about it for a moment, then said slowly, "No, please stay and get started now. I'd like the company, to be honest. The house is spooking me, on my own."

"I like a guy who can admit he's scared of ghosts," she said, and scored a laugh, which brought his whole face to life. He had the most natural, joyous laugh she'd heard from a man in a while, complete with the blink-and-you-miss-it grin he'd given a couple of minutes ago.

"You got that right!" he said frankly. "Never have been scared of 'em before. I've been in this place three months, but it's only since the shooting that I've felt—" He broke off and swore under his breath. "Don't know why I have to keep talking about it."

"We won't, then. It's a nice house," she said quickly.

"You mean it was, about eighty years ago."

"It will be again, with some work. You're having

more done than just the kitchen and the half bath, right?" She wanted to draw him out and distract him.

"Hoping to do a lot of it myself. The floors and the painting." As he talked about the renovation, he began to sound as if he was treading easier ground. He didn't look so tightly locked in embarrassment and stress. "It was my uncle's place, but he didn't live here, kept it as a rental. He left it to me when he died last year. How about some coffee, and we'll take a tour, if you'd like to see the whole place?"

Carmen saw that he sincerely wanted the distraction, the change of pace and the caffeine and said, "Yes and yes, to coffee and the tour. I'd love to see the whole house. But I'm sorry about your uncle."

"I know. He was a good guy. But he was eighty, and he'd been ill awhile." Again he seemed uncomfortable about sharing this with a stranger. She'd really got him on a bad day. The ongoing impulse to comfort him with her touch came as an irritation.

Been there, done that today. Had the embarrassment thick in the air to prove it.

And anyhow, haven't you done enough of that kind of thing in your life, Carmen O'Brien, with Dad and Melanie and Joe and Kate, and even Cormack on a bad day? All that family, needing hugs and needing you. Why go looking for more of it, just at a time where, if only Kate would settle down and find herself, you might be free?

Definitely, she wasn't going to act as Jack Davey's shoulder to cry on again today. Or, hopefully, ever.

"Want me to make the coffee?" she offered heading

through the open doorway in the direction of the fridge. "Through here?"

"No, I know where I've put everything in this mess," he answered, and followed her.

Most of the kitchen equipment had been moved into this adjoining sunroom and piled at random. The room looked as if it had once been an open porch but had been enclosed a long time ago. Even though it was a mess now, it would be a beautiful room if it had some work. Pull up the ugly indoor-outdoor carpeting, polish the floorboards…

Were there hardwood boards under here?

Carmen discreetly slid the toe of her running shoe beneath a curled-up edge of orangey-brown carpet to take a look. She loved the whole process of renovating an old house, even though she and Cormack did mostly kitchens and bathrooms. She could just imagine this room with fresh paint, comfortable furnishings, syrup-colored floorboards….

"Yeah, I took a look and it seems to be in great condition," Jack Davey said, following her downward gaze to the floor.

She hadn't been discreet enough, apparently. Felt a little shamefaced as she admitted, "I love checking out the possibilities. Cormack says I act as if every house we work on is the one I'm going to raise my kids in."

"Yeah? How many do you have?" He found the coffee jar and filters, went back into the kitchen to fill the glass pot.

"Oh, kids? None. Theoretical kids, he means." She

wasn't convinced she wanted kids of her own, actually, after she and Cormack had pretty much raised the younger three O'Brien siblings these past ten years and more. Not that her client needed to know any of that.

But maybe he'd caught something in her tone. He gave her a sideways glance and said, "Right," and the subject was closed.

He made the coffee and they drank it and munched on a Danish pastry each as they toured the sprawling house. It definitely needed work. The basement was cluttered with junk, and the dust lay thick. The washing machine down there looked like a model from the sixties. They both poked around, finding traces of damp along the north wall.

"I might have to get some new drainage in place outside." Jack bent and ran his fingers across the puckered, powdery whitewash down near floor level.

Carmen took a closer look, also, and for a moment they stood shoulder to shoulder, propping their hands on their knees as they examined the problem. "The place might just need airing out. Or you might be right and it could need more major treatment."

She was enjoying this. It reminded her of the way she and Cormack worked together, very practical and relaxed with each other. A heck of a lot easier than standing in Jack Davey's kitchen feeling him sob in her arms.

Hmm. Too relaxed, maybe.

Suddenly she felt a little self-conscious, as if she'd been standing too close. He smelled good, and that wasn't the kind of thing you should notice about a client a half hour after you first met him.

"But look at the windows," Jack said, moving away. He'd stopped favoring his injured left side now that it was hurting less, and he walked with more athletic grace than she would have expected from a lawman. He was springy on his feet, and energetic, which Carmen liked because she was energetic, too. "They're a good size. When they're clean they'll let in a lot of light, and I'll clear out the junk, paint the floor."

They went back up the rickety basement stairs. The fireplace in the living room had been closed off and replaced with an ugly gas heater, the floors needed sanding and varnishing, and you could spend three months painting the place inside and out and not have it done, but the ceilings were high and there was some great original detail. Marble and Flemish tile around the fireplace, real plaster cornices and moldings, stained and beveled glass panels beside the front door, hand carving on the hardwood newel post at the foot of the stairs.

"Want to see outside before we go upstairs?" Jack said.

"Is there much land?"

"About three-fourths of an acre. Like the house, it's a mess."

They went through a side door and around into the rear yard, where dew still lay on the untidy grass. Walking next to Jack, Carmen couldn't help taking sideways looks a couple of times. To see if he was still okay. To see what that strong, hard body really looked like, because having a man fall into her arms two minutes after she met him meant that so far she had a more vivid impression about the way he felt and smelled and sounded than about the way he looked.

Both times she found him looking back at her. A little wary, a little curious at the same time. As if he needed to check out what she really looked like, too, because he only knew about how she felt and smelled. The first time this happened, they both looked away fast. The second time, out beyond the shadow of the house, the looks held for half a second too long.

He cleared his throat. "So this is the yard." It came out a little too breezy and cheerful.

"Oh, right, great," she answered, as if she hadn't recognized that this was a yard until he said it.

When she looked closer, she saw that it was more than a yard, it was a garden. An overgrown and half-forgotten garden, but a garden all the same. She saw rosebushes that had gone unpruned for years and a stand of fruit trees that was almost an orchard. Winter-deadened weeds, creepers and sumac camouflaged an area of stone paving with a hand-chiseled birdbath at the center of it.

"It'll take work," Jack said, as if warning her.

"Yeah, I noticed," she drawled. "Are you a gardener?"

"Never have been, but when I look at this and think about the possibilities, I want to learn."

The property backed onto what was almost a cliff. Facing south, it rose forty or fifty feet, made of chunky, solid rock that was covered in a tangle of growth. In the April sun, the fresh lime-green of new leaves had begun to appear.

"This is natural, this rock face?" Carmen asked.

"That's right."

"And is that a train track up on top?"

"It's not used anymore. I climbed all the way up here one day. There are pockets of good soil in lots of places."

He paced in front of the rock face, his keenness for the project translating into energetic movement and an animated face. His eyes weren't red-rimmed anymore, and he'd begun to forget their awkward start with each other. So had Carmen. Her relief was like the April sun. Getting stronger. Warming her.

"It wouldn't be too hard to clear out this jungle and turn it into a rock garden, with creepers and flowers," he went on. "The main yard is through that hedge, to the side of the house. There are a couple of real nice trees you can see. That huge pine and the sycamore. The property goes through to this other road, here." He pointed.

A side road led to a development of new houses on a hillside, big pseudomansions made of cheap materials with no style. In Carmen's mind, even in its current dilapidated state, there was no contest between Jack's old place and those new ones. She'd take the old house every time.

"It's great," she said. "I love it. One of those times I wish C & C Renovations did the whole package, not just kitchens and bathrooms." She leaned a hand on the cool rock, closed her eyes and turned her face to the early-spring sun to absorb its rising warmth, but then she sensed how closely Jack Davey was watching her and opened her eyes to return the look.

Different from their last looks at each other. Curious, this time.

"Can I ask the obvious question now?" he said. He leaned against the rock and she thought the patch of sun would probably do his aching body some good, as well as his traumatized soul.

"Which question is that?" she asked.

"The one I'm having trouble putting into words without sounding…oh, crass, I guess."

Okay. She knew.

"You mean what's a nice girl like me doing in a renovation business like this?"

"That's the one. Sorry."

"Yeah. Don't go all macho and chauvinistic on me, okay?" she blurted out.

"I'm trying not to. But it is a little unusual. Does everyone hit you with it?"

"Or they hit my brother with it. They wonder if I'm going to pull my weight. But then we point out that we work on a contract basis, not by the hour, so if my dainty hand is too feeble to lift a hammer, it costs us, not the client."

"Which doesn't tell me why you went into it in the first place."

"Family reasons, mostly." He wouldn't want the details. She found herself giving too many of them, anyhow. For some reason, he seemed easy to talk to. "We needed a business where Cormack could use his building skills and I could train with him while we worked. We didn't have a lot of capital to invest. There was no money for more education. We had to be able to get off the ground fast. It was tough at first. We had small jobs, with a lot of gaps between them. But then we started getting good references from the work we'd done, and now we sometimes have to turn clients away."

Although she'd summarized extensively, she wished she'd been briefer. He wasn't the only one spilling too much information and too much emotion this morning.

"And you like hammering?" He seemed to be mentally contrasting this unlikely personality trait with the traits in other women he'd known, and he wasn't getting a match.

Curvy girl bits. Hammering. Dangly earrings. Toolbox with pry bar.

She *liked* hammering?

Shouldn't she prefer to be shoe shopping at the mall?

"I like knowing how to do it right," she said, deciding to trust him with the truth. "There's a satisfaction in getting the rhythm and hitting the sweet spot, feeling the nail go in like a knife through butter. And I like creating a kitchen or a bathroom that works, as well as looking good. If you want, you can call that the feminine touch. For some clients, it's one of C & C's selling points. That I have a woman's eye for where to put the utensil drawer and the hooks for the pot holders."

He laughed. "I didn't even know the second half of C & C was female when I talked to your brother."

"Yeah, that can work pretty well for us, too," she drawled deliberately.

They looked away from each other again.

"Want to go back in and see upstairs?"

"Maybe you'll want C & C to tackle the upstairs bathroom next, so I should take a look." At this stage, they were only contracted to do the kitchen and half-bath downstairs.

He led the way back inside and up to the master bedroom, where his T-shirt drawer hung open with a mess of fabric spilling out. The sight reminded them both of how he'd greeted her an hour ago and what had happened next. He went to shut it, but an awkwardness had come back into the atmosphere now, and the rest of his tour was sketchy and brief.

"We should both probably do some work if we're going to get much done this morning," he said.

"Yes, or I'll have to answer to Cormack as soon as he's better. I'm not expecting you to help, though, seriously."

"That's okay. Got a project of my own."

Turned out he was preparing to paint the sunroom today, keeping the horrible carpet in place to protect the floor. They arrived back in the kitchen, and with misgivings, she watched him climb a stepladder and start scraping the ceiling. "Are you fit enough for that, Jack? Your chest, I mean."

"I'll stop if it starts hurting. You're right, though, I couldn't help you pull out those old cabinets, judging from how much it seemed to tear me up, coming too fast down the stairs."

Carmen had begun working on the cabinets with a pry bar. They weren't original to the house and weren't worth saving. The green laminated particle board had swollen out of shape in numerous places, and it was ugly and cheap to begin with.

"Rob should be here sometime this morning to help with the heavy work," she said. Several nails screeched as the pry bar pulled a strip of wood loose. She added without thinking, "But I'm not as much of a girl as I look."

From his position on the stepladder, Jack Davey twisted around and looked at her, long and slow. "What's wrong with being a girl?" he said, his gray eyes teasing and thoughtful and steady at the same time, and that was the moment Carmen first began to understand that she could be in real trouble, that Jack Davey knew it, and that he could be in trouble, too.

The twisting motion on the stepladder had not been a good idea, Jack soon realized. The surgically repaired mess under his left rib cage burned again. Carmen saw him wince and heard the hitch in his breathing.

"Don't say it," he warned. "You're right. I'm going to call the doctor, see if he can squeeze me into his appointment hours to check this out. It keeps happening, and it probably shouldn't."

"Are you supposed to be driving yet?"

"No. Wanna call me a cab?"

"I was going to offer to *be* the cab."

"That works, too, if you don't mind doing it."

"I'm getting the impression today's going to be slow for C & C Renovations."

"Add the extra time into your invoice." He looked down at his chest. "I'd better change my shirt. Again."

The receptionist at Dr. Seeger's put him through to the doctor himself, who sounded concerned. "You're right. I should take a look. You're not doing anything stupid, are you?"

"Maybe I'd better not answer that. What would you say, just hypothetically, if I told you I was doing paint preparation in my sunroom?"

The doctor sighed down the phone. "Didn't we go over this in the hospital?"

"You said nothing strenuous. I'm right-handed, and the shot went in on the left. When the pain first tweaked this morning, all I was doing was coming down the stairs a little too fast."

"I'll fit you in as soon as you get here."

They took the C & C pickup truck. Jack liked the way Carmen drove. She was a little sassy at the wheel, delivering sarcastic one-liners to any idiots on the road, but with a thread of humor in the mix that toned it down. She had the windows shut, too, so no one would hear.

"I hope your eyebrows get painted on crooked, lady!" she yelled at a woman who was applying her makeup at the traffic lights and who clearly found the process far more interesting than checking the color of the lights. "Green means go, honey, green means go, say it after me," she chanted, until the vehicle in front finally moved. Then she turned to Jack. "Tell me to shut up if you hate this," she said. "Cormack often does. Even though he knows it helps my sanity."

"You need help with your sanity?"

She shrugged and grinned, and her red earrings

swung against her tanned neck. "Life gets complicated. I'm the go-to girl in the O'Brien family and my baby sister is being a pain in the butt right now—she's just turned eighteen. Helps to yell at idiots in traffic instead of yelling at her."

"I can relate to that," he said, thinking of Terri and her new husband, and the ice junkie with the crazy gun. "Sometimes you need to off-load stuff onto someone safe."

"Yeah," she said quietly, as if she'd understood his thoughts. "Um, are you going to ask the doctor about that, too? I mean, about…"

"Crying on your shoulder?" He raked his teeth over his lower lip, a little scared that even just saying the words might bring those hair-trigger emotions bubbling back up.

"Yep. That." She glanced across at him, must have seen the way his face had gone tight. She added lightly, "Not that your tears have ruined my gorgeous silk blouse or anything." She fingered her plain cotton T-shirt.

The humor helped. "I'll buy you a new one in gold satin," he promised. "You want C & C Renovations embroidered on the pocket, like on that one?"

"Seriously, though…"

"How about if we're not?" he said quickly. "Serious, I mean. I'll ask the doctor. He knows I'm seeing the counselor and taking time off."

"Okay. Just wanted to check."

"Well, thanks, but I think I have a handle on this."

She made a tricky lane change in silence, then asked, "And your partner, how's he doing?"

"He took a vacation with his wife to Bermuda. She's great. Down to earth. Says she's planning to come home pregnant. Her dad's a cop, too. Russ'll be okay."

"He didn't get shot."

"The getting shot is the least of it. It's the shooting someone else that breaks you up."

"I can imagine."

"Here's the doctor's building coming up on the right, after the next light. There's parking out front. You can wait in the pickup, if you want. Hopefully this won't take long."

"Hmm, wait in the pickup... Does this doctor have good magazines? Or just ones with fish and cars on the covers?"

"What's wrong with fish and cars?"

"Despite the toolbox, I am actually a girl, Jack," she drawled. "I believe we've already covered that? I gotta catch up on my celebrity gossip or I grow forests of unwanted body hair overnight."

He laughed. "No forests. He has good magazines."

"Then I'll come in and read."

They waited five minutes before Dr. Seeger called him in, and he left Carmen with her pile of glitzy reading.

"Okay," the doctor said, sounding way too eager. "Let's see if I can cause some pain."

Bottom line, he could.

Other than that, the news was good.

"I don't think you've caused any further damage," Dr. Seeger said. "Your blood pressure is normal and your temperature, your heart. There's no sign of infection or swelling. It wasn't hurting until I poked at it just now?"

"No, but if I twist…"

"Don't twist. You're, what, ten days out of surgery? You're still healing. Go easy on this."

"Do I have to lie down?"

"Not unless you want to. Have you been taking your pain medication?"

"I stopped it. Made my head too fuzzy and I hated it."

The doctor fixed him with a thoughtful look. "It's probably good that you've stopped, although I wouldn't recommend that strategy to every patient. You're the type who thinks he's cured if he can't feel actual pain. The hero type. If you pop painkillers, who knows what you'll do to yourself and never realize."

They negotiated Jack's exact level of permitted activity for a couple more minutes, and Jack wondered if maybe this "hero-type" thing had some truth to it. Dr. Seeger certainly seemed able to predict a few of his recent behavior patterns with a high degree of accuracy. There was also the lingering suggestion that the "hero" label wasn't one hundred percent complimentary.

He left the doctor's office with mixed feelings.

"He says I can keep painting," Jack reported when he got back to Carmen in the waiting room. He looked pleased and a little thoughtful.

"Is that good?"

"Hell, yeah!"

"What else did he say?" She put down her magazines

and stood up, sensing he was eager to get out of there. The car keys in his hand provided a tiny clue. He was jiggling them impatiently, even though they belonged to his own car, not the C & C pickup that they'd arrived in, and he wasn't even driving.

"What else?" he echoed. "Good blood pressure, no infection or swelling. And he says I should go easy on the painkillers because I'm the—" He stopped.

"The what?" she prompted.

"Nah. Nothing."

"Go on. Worst patient he's ever had? Rarest blood group on the planet?"

He shrugged, tucked in the corner of his mouth and spread his hands. "The hero type. For what it's worth."

What was it worth?

Carmen didn't know.

She didn't have a lot of experience with heroes.

## Chapter Three

Four days of solid work later—a lot of splintered wood, a lot of paint fumes, a lot of dirt and mess, the occasional presence of Rob to help with the heavy work, not much conversation—Carmen flipped her cell phone shut and announced to Jack, "That was Cormack. He and Rob should be here with the new kitchen cabinets in about a half hour. They've hit a delay at the warehouse, but they're sorting it out."

"No problem," Jack answered easily.

He had seemed more relaxed as each day passed. His side looked to be hurting him less, and he'd told her that Ryan was coming tonight, for the first of his more-frequent weekends here. Carmen could see Jack was happy about it, but a little wound up at the same time. He'd looked at his watch several times over the past hour.

"At least, it's no problem for me," he added. "Do you have somewhere you need to be?"

"No, I'll wait. We won't get any of the cabinets put in tonight, but they'll take a while to unload from the truck, and we'll want to check them for any damage or anything that's wrong. Will it be a problem if we're still here when Ryan arrives, though?"

He looked at his watch again. "Shouldn't be."

But he frowned. Carmen already had the impression that his ex's reactions could be unpredictable.

It was late Friday afternoon and almost dark out. Chilly, too, with so many windows open to air out the smell of fresh paint. Jack had almost finished the sunroom. He'd been working with a roller at the far end, rapidly filling in the last sections with long, smooth strokes.

Carmen watched him as he returned to the work. He leaned down to the roller tray, still favoring his injured side a little. He put the roller against the wall and pushed up and down, and the muscle in his upper right arm went a little harder and rounder, below the loose band of that frayed old T-shirt, which was now splattered with paint. The color went onto the wall with a hissy, splishy kind of sound, and Jack hummed a couple of bars of a classic rock riff under his breath, sounding a little on edge after the mention of Ryan's arrival. "Dunh, dunh, *da,* dunh, dunh, dunh-*da.*"

She recognized what he was humming. Deep Purple. "Smoke on the Water."

He'd done a good job, her professional eye told her. Most amateur painters skimped on the prep work. They didn't spend enough time sanding or filling in holes, didn't tape the windows, and ended up with sloppy edges and rough spots. Jack hadn't even opened his paint cans until yesterday evening, after she and Rob had gone for the day. He must have worked for hours last night on the ceiling, and today he'd done the main wall color, a buttery cream. There was a contrasting trim to go on later, in a pale Wedgwood-blue.

"I like it," she told him. Then she fought a yawn, which Jack fortunately missed.

If he'd spent half last night painting, she'd spent at least as much time worrying about Kate being out late again, and listening for the sound of her coming through the front door. She'd heard her sister's key in the lock at almost two, and then unsteady footsteps stumbling up the stairs.

"Yeah? You do?" He turned. "I wanted to prep it well enough so it didn't need a second coat. Really wanted it done today, before—" He stopped. "Well, just done today. What do you think?"

"You'll have to wait for brighter light, but I can't see any patchy spots. You may have some touching up, that's all."

"And it's not too yellow?"

"Not at all," she reassured him.

"And not too, you know, girly?"

"Not to my eye."

"Good."

He wanted the new paint job to be finished enough to show off to Ryan, she realized, and he wanted Ryan to like it. This was no bachelor pad he was creating for himself, here. He wanted it to be a home.

"A sunroom has to be sunny," she said. "You can tone down the cheeriness with some darker furnishings. It's not girly." His concern for Ryan's opinion reminded her of her own concern over Kate, and that she should call and let her know she'd be late home for dinner, because of Cormack's delay. "And of course when the trim and floor are done it'll look so different, and so much better," she told him. "Really impressive. Great room for a kid's computer and study desk."

"You think so?" He looked happy at the idea.

"Definitely, when it's all finished."

He grinned. "I'm going to enjoy throwing this carpet into a Dumpster."

"I'll bet!"

She made the call to Kate but was asked to "Please leave a message" on both the land line at home and Kate's cell. "Hi, Kate, it's me," she told the cell phone. "Wanna cook something, if you get in? There's pasta and salad fixings, deli pasta sauce in the refrigerator. I'll be there for it, but late. Cormack won't be. Anyhow, call me when you get this, okay? Let me know what's happening."

*She's eighteen, she's college age, she's not a child,* ran the familiar mantra in her head, after she put down the phone. The mantra didn't help. Nothing helped. Kate was a mess. She'd broken up with her boyfriend a month ago, and even though Mitchell had been a jerk and bad news and not nearly good enough for Kate, she still had a wounded heart. Carmen was scared. Their talks achieved nothing.

Cormack had no solutions to offer, either. He tended to opt out by spending his evenings elsewhere, leaving Carmen to fret and yell and try a new strategy with Kate every week. Sometimes she got angry with her older brother and business partner, but he was probably right when he said that there was nothing they could do. Kate had to ride out her own problems, deal with her own heartaches and learn from her own mistakes.

Restless and concerned, Carmen wandered into the sunroom to watch Jack fill in the last unpainted rectangle of wall. "Want some help cleaning your gear?" she asked him, unhappy about the circular motion of her thoughts about her sister. "There's nothing more I can do until Cormack and Rob get here."

"You don't have to help. You look pretty wiped."

"I hate sitting around."

Because then I'm just going to either A, worry about Kate or B, spend too much time watching the way Jack's butt looks in those old jeans when he moves.

Yeah, definitely she was in trouble.

And though a part of her sang out a warning that she should run a mile, because she had no time for a man, especially a man with a nine-year-old son, when she had Kate to worry about and Melanie and Joe only just grown and gone, another part of her insisted, *Isn't it time I had something for me?*

Jack Davey would most definitely be something for *her.*

Which part of herself did she listen to? The sensible, nurturing part, or the part that wanted to take a leaf out of Kate's book and throw caution to the four winds, right along with her tender heart?

"If you're serious, start on the trim brushes," Jack said, pulling them from the plastic bag he'd stored them in to stop them from drying out. "I'm done with them. Use that old sink in the basement."

"Sure." She reached out and he gave them to her, the two handles inevitably sticky with paint drips that had run down them. She was accustomed to messy hands. His were stained and sticky, also, and when their fingers touched as she took the brushes, the stickiness glued them together for a moment. She didn't try too hard to pull away.

"How fast does this stuff dry?" she murmured, and he favored her with his blink-and-you-miss-it grin.

"Fast," he said. "Better go wash it off." He dropped his voice. "Your hands are too pretty to have paint all over 'em."

Yep. Serious trouble. What kind of signal had she sent just then?

Down in the basement she ran water over the brushes and squeezed the thick bristles, knowing she'd probably still have paint traces on her hands a couple of days from now, despite the industrial-strength soap she and Cormack kept at home.

The water was beginning to flow clearer when Jack came down with the roller. She heard his footsteps on the old wooden stairs and her heart began to beat faster. It was pretty shadowy down here. Atmospheric. A little more dangerous, in all sorts of ways, than being alone with him in the kitchen and sunroom while they worked.

She stepped sideways to give him room, and he used her almost-clean waste water to rinse away the thickest of the paint on the roller. "Those are about done, aren't they?" he said, after a while.

She looked at her brushes. They were. For a good minute she'd just been standing here wondering why it felt so nice to have Jack Davey this close, and what one of them might do about it. She knew he felt this chemistry, too…

"Here's a rag for drying them." He reached up to a nail sticking out from the wooden floor beam above their heads and pulled down what had to be another one of his old T-shirts. Their arms bumped. He shut off the faucet.

When she took the rag from him, he didn't let it go. She pulled. He tugged gently back. She looked up at him. "Thanks for saying the right things about the paint," he said.

"That's okay. It does look good." She added, "But I know why it's important. You want Ryan to like it."

"Oh, I'm that transparent?"

"Maybe because I'm that way with my baby sister, sometimes. Thinking—oh, too much, probably—about what I can do to make her happy. I recognized what you felt. Ryan comes first."

"That's right. I say that to myself all the time. In exactly those words."

He still hadn't let go of the rag. Carmen stopped pulling. They both just stood and looked at each other, while he dried their wet hands on the soft, stretchy fabric. Finally, he dropped the rag into the sink and looked at what he'd done. Two sets of clean, dry, pink hands, the big, strong pair cradling the smaller, work-hardened pair.

"Much prettier," he said softly.

"They're not," she stammered. "They're not proper girl hands at all. They have cuts on them, sometimes, and scars. I use creams and stuff, but—"

He cut her off. "They're sexy as hell."

"Yeah?"

"Yeah. Because they're real. Sexiest girl hands I've ever seen."

As if to prove it, he lifted them and kissed them, then took his lips away, laced his fingers through hers and kissed her mouth. It was the second time in three days that she'd found herself in Jack Davey's arms, only this time no one was crying.

He kept his fingers threaded in hers, dropping their arms to their sides. His lips brushed her mouth, taking it slow. "Is this okay?" he muttered.

"Yes," she whispered back. Because it was most definitely okay, so why pretend differently?

The single word was all it took. He deepened the kiss at once, pulling her hard against him, parting her lips with his, tasting her, turning her mouth delectably numb and tingling. He kissed like a dream, kissed from the heart, kissed as if the world might end tonight, and that was just the way she wanted it. Good, and unashamed.

Instinctively she lifted one hand into his hair and caressed the clean, silky strands. She'd done this four days ago. Different reason. Just as good. They knew each other better now. How did that happen to two people? It was strange. Making coffee for each other while they worked. A few casual lines about measurements and cabinets and paint colors.

But somehow, thanks to tears and embarrassment and coffee and paint colors, she knew him and he felt right. Right beneath the touch of her fingers, right to her sense of taste and smell, the right heat radiating from his strong body, the right words whispered in her ear.

"On Monday morning…" he said. Kisses and words. She could barely tell the difference. "Even when I was…" his breath touched her lips. His mouth was like poetry "…sobbing like a baby on your shoulder, I loved how you felt. I hit you with all of that emotion…"

"It was okay. I could see how it just washed over you."

"You were great. The fact that you didn't run screaming…"

"I've had some practice."

"Yeah?"

"Family."

"Why are we talking about this?"

"We're not."

"Good…" he said, and the word drowned itself against her mouth.

He kissed her hard, ran his hands down her back and over her rear end, shaping her curves, coming up to lift her hair from her neck and make sensual touch patterns against her nape and behind her ears. She felt the press of her breasts against him, and the growing ridge of his arousal against her stomach. They were the wrong size for each other but it didn't matter a bit. They still fit, somehow. He bent and she stretched. It was just…right.

And then it was interrupted.

Carmen heard the pop of car tires on the tarred driveway at the side of the house, right next to the windows above the old sink.

Cormack and Rob, with the cabinets.

Jack muttered something under his breath, and if it was a curse word, then Carmen fully agreed.

She didn't want this to stop. How could she stop?

But the sound of the arrival had cut jaggedly into their kiss like a knife cutting tough steak, and she felt Jack start to let go. His hands showed his reluctance. So did his mouth. She felt his hot touch, first against her back then dropping to her hips. His kiss trailed across her jaw and down her neck, warm and giving and alive, promising more, promising later.

It was only the promise of later that allowed her to let go now. How crazy was that?

"This must be Cormack," she said, breathless.

And maybe his timing was fortunate because the implications of kissing Jack were looming larger by the second. That other part of her was talking louder, the part she hadn't listened to before, the part that said nothing about how this could possibly work, when Ryan came first in his life, and Kate's current problems came first in hers, and what Carmen wanted most in the world right

now was to be free of such a heavy weight of responsibility.

"I guess," he said, about Cormack.

"Finish cleaning the roller?" she prompted him.
"We'll be a while, unloading."

He grabbed her hand and squeezed it and they looked
at each other helplessly for a moment.

"Jack, maybe we should…"

"Go," he said. "We can't talk now."

"No. I know." Her body throbbed and burned as she
hurried up the stairs. She smoothed her hair and her
shirt, knowing Cormack would have questions about her
flushed face and bright eyes. He'd probably think *Difficult client,* not *Kissing by the basement sink,* because
difficult clients were far, far more common than clients
who even looked as if they might touch a woman the
way Jack Davey did.

Would her brother ask her about it?

Cool down, she coached herself. Don't let him see
that something happened.

She went directly to the side entrance, where
Cormack and Rob should just about be standing by now.
There was no one there, so she went to the front of the
house, yanked the big, ill-fitting door open and found a
petite, blue-eyed blonde standing on the porch with her
mouth already pursed in impatience at how long she'd
had to stand waiting.

Oh. Right.

"You must be Terri," Carmen said, sounding a little
too abrupt.

Jack's ex.

She saw a boy with Jack's dark hair and a slight but wiry build coming up the saggy old steps with a backpack slung on one shoulder. Ryan—number-one priority in Jack Davey's life. To both mother and son she said, "Come in."

The purse on Terri's lips gathered tighter, as she looked Carmen up and down. "Jack didn't say he'd have someone here."

She said *someone* as if it meant *call girl,* or at the very best, *sleazy new squeeze,* but Carmen understood how a mother might have concerns about a possible unknown new girlfriend in her son's father's life. She explained quickly, "I'm not someone. I'm completely not anybody at all. I'm just remodeling his kitchen." *And if my cheeks are on fire, then they're lying!* "I actually thought you were going to be the rest of the team, bringing the new cabinets."

Terri didn't seem interested in the new cabinets, let alone Carmen herself, now that she'd turned out to be the hired help. "But he's home?" She didn't wait for an answer, just marched into the house. "Jack?" she called sweetly. "This is a little inappropriate, isn't it?"

*Inappropriate.* Such a falsely sanitary word. It came out of Terri's mouth with vinegar flavoring, and Carmen already understood quite a lot about why Terri and Jack were divorced.

She focused on Ryan, instead. He looked so much like Jack, down to the same expression on his face—a mix of anticipation and wariness. It melted her heart. This was a fresh start for him, too, in his relationship with his dad, and he was a little wary. "Hi," she said brightly. She knew about fresh starts in families. "I'm Carmen. Want to put your backpack by the stairs or something? It looks heavy."

Terri turned back to her. "Didn't you say you were from the construction crew?"

"Yes, that's right," Carmen confirmed helpfully, since apparently she hadn't been clear enough before.

"Hmm." Terri's look said that a kitchen remodeler making suggestions to a nine-year-old about where he could put his backpack was almost as "inappropriate" as the remodeler answering the door in the first place.

Jack had appeared. "We thought you were the cabinets," he said to Terri.

"Didn't I say we'd be here by six?"

He looked at his watch. "And it's a quarter after. Which was about when we were expecting Cormack and Rob with the cabinets."

Carmen heard another vehicle engine outside. "This is Cormack and Rob," she said quickly. "No problem." She went out to the porch and found that Terri's car was blocking the truck's continuation down the driveway. For convenience and speed, they needed to unload directly through the side door. She added apologetically, "Um, Terri, unless you're leaving right away, I'll have to ask you to move your car."

With exaggerated patience, Terri held the keys out to Carmen at arm's length. "Have you ever driven a BMW?" Her face said she doubted it, and she turned away without waiting for a reply.

Carmen held the keys, thinking sarcastically, *Oh yeah, I run around in them all the time, stick shift and automatic, all makes and models, every color of the rainbow.*

It was official.

She didn't like Jack's ex.

She was tempted to say out loud, I'm pretty good in a Mercedes or a Lamborghini, too. But she heroically managed to keep the lines purely in her thoughts.

Terri must be a mind-reader, however, because she almost looked as if she was about to snatch back the keys. On the way out the door to move the vehicle, Carmen heard her say, "I really don't think this is appropriate for Ryan, Jack, for you to have a work crew in the house while he's here."

"It's six-fifteen on a Friday. They won't be here long."

In the driveway, Carmen signaled to Cormack and Rob that she was moving the car, reversed out toward the mailbox, then angled the vehicle onto the unkempt stretch of grass in front of the house. They drove the truck farther in and began to unload the cabinets, keeping the protective packaging in place and setting everything down in the dining room. Cormack was still taking cold and flu medication, but he was a lot better than he'd been earlier in the week.

In the living room Terri and Jack were still talking.

"Go on upstairs, Ryan, honey," Carmen heard Terri say, and, as soon as his footsteps sounded overhead, in quite a different tone, "This arrangement can be changed if it doesn't work out, Jack, you know that, don't you?"

"Of course I know that. And it cuts both ways."

"What could you possibly mean by that?"

"Never mind, it's nothing."

"No, Jack. I want an explanation."

"Well, let's just say if you open a nude-mud-wrestling venue in your pool cabana, I might have a case for full-time custody."

"That's ridiculous! And totally inappropriate!"

"No, it's a joke, because I'm trying to keep this light. Terri, I really don't think that having a couple of people here unloading kitchen cabinets on a Friday evening is going to traumatize our son."

"No, but it's going to rob him of your attention."

"Which you've been doing ever since we first separated three years ago, by not letting me have more time with him, so please don't try that argument."

Carmen went back out to the truck to bring in the new stainless steel sink, but her cell phone rang in her back pocket on the way.

Kate.

She came around to the front of the house and sat on the porch steps for some privacy and tried to sound as upbeat as possible. "Hi, Katie-girl!"

"I'm home and there's no dinner, so I'm—"

"But did you get my message? I'll be home in a bit. And there's fresh pasta and deli sauce, one of those creamy ones you like."

"I'm not going to wait. I'm going out. Courtney's picking me up. Well, her boyfriend."

"Courtney's boyfriend is picking you up. Where are you going?"

"Just out."

"Is there a plan?"

"Just out, Carmen!"

"Wait, okay? I'll be there in ten minutes." Well, twenty, at least, but if she said twenty she knew Kate wouldn't even consider waiting. On the other hand, if she didn't keep to her golden rule of honesty with her baby sister, then what was left? "Actually, not ten, I guess. Longer. But I'd like to eat with you."

This was honest.

And I don't want you out drinking again, especially not on an empty stomach. You're under the legal drinking age for another two years and ten months!

Which was even more honest, but blatantly counter-productive, so she kept it to herself.

"I hate cooking," Kate whined, her voice rising in volume and pitch. "I mean, you're not here, Carmen, the house is cold and dark, and now I have to cook, too? I've been serving burgers all day." Kate had dropped out of college a few months ago, and was working at a local fast-food place almost full-time. Her pay was the pits. "I stink of them. If I don't hit the shower in thirty seconds, I'm going to throw up. And I'm not staying to eat with you. I'm going out. You only want me at home because you don't like Courtney's boyfriend and you don't want him picking me up."

"That's not true!"

Carmen heard footsteps behind her, and Terri's voice. "If you could excuse me?" She shifted her backside from the center of the steps to the side, and Terri passed.

"Kate, why do you make this complicated when it's simple? Let's just eat together before you go out, okay? I love you."

Terri turned in the driveway with another of her disapproving looks. Apparently this phone conversation was inappropriate, also. Was it because of the emotional tone? Because Carmen was sitting on the steps? Was she holding the cell phone to an inappropriate ear?

"Listen," she said to her sister, as the BMW left the driveway. "I am leaving here in three minutes. I will cook the pasta. I will make my Ten-Minute Tiramisu recipe for dessert." She closed her eyes, ashamed of herself. What did parenting books say about using bribery on kids? And they were usually talking about two-year-olds. "If you are not there when I get home, I love you anyway."

Kate disconnected the call.

## Chapter Four

Carmen O'Brien had beautiful eyes, twinkling and chocolate brown and alive.

When she came back into the house, they were clouded with worry, and Jack wanted to ask her what was wrong.

He wanted to ask her a whole lot of things, actually.

Was Terri being a witch to you?

Did you love that kiss as much as I did?

When can I see you again? Can we dress up a little and go out somewhere, and could it have nothing to do with hammers and paint?

But Cormack had questions about the cabinets, and Ryan needed settling in. He would be hungry any minute, if he wasn't already. There was no time for Jack to follow through on what had happened with the two of them just now in the basement. Carmen went to slip past him in the direction of the kitchen and he stopped her with a quick touch on her arm. "You okay?"

"I'm fine." She looked up at him, earrings long and delicate against her neck, eyes very dark. "My baby sister's being a pain in the butt, that's all."

She leaned a little closer than she really needed to. It was more like a sway than a lean, as if she didn't know it was happening and wasn't fully in control. His breath caught in his throat for a moment, frozen by the strength of the pull between them. He could almost see it shimmering in the air. He could feel it on his skin, in the beat of his heart and in the weight of his groin.

"I have a couple of those," he told her, struggling to focus. "Pain-in-the-butt baby sisters, I mean. They live in Florida, not far from my mom and dad. Both married with kids." For some reason he wanted the two of them to pour out their life stories to each other, this minute.

"I wish my sister lived in Florida." She looked up at him, half smiling but not really seeing him anymore, Jack thought. Her sister held the prime position in her thoughts, and he wondered about their relationship. "Florida. Alaska. Greenland. The moon. But she's only eighteen so I can't get rid of her just yet."

She sounded grim about it, but then she sighed and he picked up on the care that lay beneath her words. The care and the aura of responsibility. Why was that? Didn't the O'Briens have parents?

Suddenly he had a whole lot more questions for her.

"Dad?" *Speaking of parents...* "Are we gonna eat soon?" Ryan asked. "I'm hungry. Like, *starving* hungry."

With the kitchen out of action, Jack hadn't been able to stock up on good kid food. He'd been holding his breath, waiting for Terri's criticism on the issue, and he'd marshaled his defense ahead of time. He had set up a camp stove in the living room, and they were having home-cooked chicken burgers tonight, with non-negotiable lettuce and grated carrot in the filling.

He hated feeling that he had so much to prove. He'd spent the past ten years, almost, being the best father he could. Why did Terri always assume that he was going to feed their son nothing but junk? Why did she always act as if she was the only one who cared about his well-being?

Jack had broken off a promising relationship with a woman several months ago because the career-oriented fellow police officer hadn't understood his need to see more of his son. A huge motivation in his hard work on this house was to have a great place for Ryan to call his second home—a place that had mess and warmth and welcome, more than the pristine surfaces and in-your-face luxury Terri loved. As Carmen had said less than half an hour ago, down in his shadowy basement, Ryan came first.

Why did Terri always act as if that wasn't true?

He told Ryan about the dinner plan, and Ryan went, "Yay! Burgers!"

"Want to help cook? We're kind of camping this weekend, until the kitchen's back up and running. Let me just talk to Cormack for a couple of minutes, then we'll get started."

Carmen had gone through into the kitchen end of the house while Jack had been distracted by the state of Ryan's stomach, and he ached with frustration when he heard her voice in conversation with her brother. They had a lot of unfinished business. That hadn't felt like a throwaway kiss, standing by the basement sink, their hands joined together with a paint-stained rag.

It was more important than that.

It needed action.

But Ryan needed action, too. "You're not going to talk to him for too long, are you? Like when Mom says two minutes, and then it goes for twenty?"

"I'll try, buddy."

"Because I have important stuff to talk about, too. I want to get a dog, Dad," he burst out suddenly, as if he'd been waiting for weeks to say the words and couldn't wait a second longer. "A puppy. Like, for my birthday." He would turn ten in a couple of months. "But Jay says it's not the Kruger way, to just ask for stuff and get it. That I have to earn it. I have to get straight As and pass my music exam. Is that the Davey way, too? Do I have to earn a dog? We were all set to get one when I was little, but then…"

He'd been six, Jack remembered, going on seven, and yes, they had talked about a puppy, but then Terri had announced that she wanted a separation and…yeah. The timing was too wrong.

And now Ryan was caught between the Kruger way

and the Davey way and, shoot, what was Jack going to do about it? As usual, he didn't like the way Terri and Jay had handled the issue. He could agree with a kid needing to earn the latest expensive electronic gaming system by getting good grades, but a puppy? Wasn't a dog a kind of birthright for a child, as long as you had a decent yard to put it in and the time to take care of it?

"We'll talk about it as soon as I'm done with Mr. O'Brien," he said, squeezing Ryan's shoulder.

He managed to finish with Cormack in four minutes, while Rob and Carmen completed a check of what they'd unloaded. Jack and Ryan were fully absorbed in flipping the chicken burgers in a skillet over the blue gas flame when C & C Renovations announced that they were through for the week and would be back first thing Monday morning.

"See you, Jack," Carmen said, appearing briefly in the living-room doorway.

"Yeah," he answered. "Have a good night."

They smiled at each other, but then she flicked her gaze away and touched her fingers to her hair, tilting her chin like a shy animal. Her cheeks had gone pink. Jack wasn't sure what he should think about her reaction, but planned to bite the bullet until he could and find out.

From her position in front of the kitchen stove at noon on Saturday—cleaning it, sadly, not removing something delicious from the oven—Carmen covertly watched Kate thump with bare, unsteady feet down the stairs in a pair of saggy pink pj's, then cross the small front hallway. The squeak of protesting springs told her that her baby sister had arrived at the couch and there her progress had ceased.

The TV started up. Snatched jumbles of sound indicated that channel surfing was in progress. The noise settled into the exaggerated voice tones and stylized sound effects of a Japanese cartoon. Carmen heard Kate giggling. Under the guise of collecting a couple of dirty coffee cups from the end table, she took a better look.

Yep.

Her eighteen-year-old sister was sprawled out on the couch watching Saturday cartoons at noon on a beautiful spring day, with her hair a mess and her face bleary and… "I can put those pj's in the laundry, if you want," Carmen offered, because even from a distance of six feet, she could tell they really needed it.

"They're fine. I'm fine. It's fine, Carmie."

"What are you *eating?*"

Kate shrugged and held up a giant, half-empty pack of pink marshmallows. "Breakfast."

"Kate—"

"Don't start, Carmen." The tone was aggressive and cold. Kate picked up the book that was open and face-down on her stomach. She disappeared into it, looking deeply focused, with a gesture that said, "If you think I'm ignoring you, you're right."

Reading.

Reading was good.

"*What* are you reading?"

Kate held up the book. The cover design looked amateurish, and the binding had broken at the back. *Growing African Violets* read the title. "It's hysterical," Kate said. "Someone left it on a table." At the fast-food place, Carmen understood. "It is the most earnest, boring, pointless piece of badly written, badly spelled literature I have ever read in my life, it is sooo funny! This woman must have paid to have it printed out of her own pocket."

She laughed unkindly. She was a very bright girl who was doing absolutely nothing with her own gifted brain, so she entertained herself by mocking others with lesser gifts. Carmen had a strong suspicion that she did it because she was unhappy and bored, but Kate would never listen to such a bossy-older-sister theory if she dared to present it. Now she yawned, ate another marshmallow, put the book back on her stomach and turned her attention to the TV.

"So you're not really reading it," Carmen said unwisely. "You're just—"

"Yeah, completely wasting my time. What a shocking abuse of a young life." Kate rolled her eyes. The phone rang. "That's probably, like, Courtney or someone. Are you getting it, Carmen?" she said, her voice languid and apathetic.

Well, yeah. Because it'll have switched to the answer machine by the time you've thought about lifting your butt off that couch, Katie.

Frustrated, Carmen hurried back to the kitchen and snatched the phone off its mounting on the wall. "Hello?"

"Um, hi. Is that Carmen? It's Jack. Jack Davey."

Oh.

Heat flooded her at once.

"Hi. Um, yes, this is Carmen. Hi, Jack."

So far, a scintillating exchange.

His voice sounded gravelly and warm and just a little uncertain, which made something dangerous go *twang* in her heart. Remembering yesterday's kiss and a whole workweek of sneaking looks at his strong, wounded body, listening to the way he hummed under his breath while he worked, watching his fingers curl around a coffee mug, she couldn't seem to breathe right.

And what the heck had happened to her knees?

"I was wondering…" Jack said.

But Kate had turned the TV up louder, or else the cartoon violence had reached a new peak of frenzy. Carmen put a hand over her free ear and headed for the kitchen door, missing most of his next sentence. She made a couple of encouraging, "Mmm" sounds, so he would know she was still here.

"…thinking dinner," she heard, as she reached the back steps and sat down.

"I'm sorry?"

"You're going to make me say it again, aren't you?"

"Um, because my sister has the TV on and I didn't hear that last bit."

Or that first bit, to be honest.

"I said I was thinking dinner, but you know, it's up to you. Just a drink or a movie."

"Actually, Jack, I didn't really hear any of it."

I think you're asking me out. I think that's why there

was that cute, uncertain kind of rush in your words when you started. But women have their uncertainties, too. That you're asking me out is not the kind of assumption a girl wants to make in error, and I need time to work out my answer anyhow.

Time to breathe.

Time to decide how sensible I am.

Or how selfish.

And the significance of these jellied knees.

"Can you start again?" she asked. Her skin prickled with another flare of heat.

She heard Kate behind her in the kitchen, opening and closing cupboards and freezer and refrigerator doors, on the prowl for something more filling than marshmallows for breakfast.

Which was good, except that she'd probably find Cormack's doughnuts....

"Ohh, chocolate glazed!" Kate exclaimed.

She'd found them. Nutritionally, they weren't much of an improvement on her previous choice.

"Maybe I'm way off base, here," Jack said, down the phone. His words were overtaken by a loud clatter at his end, and the sounds of a nine-year-old boy trying not to swear.

"Ouch!" Carmen heard. "Shoot! Ouch, ouch!"

"Excuse me for a second," Jack said "Ryan, hell, what are you doing?" His words sounded a little muffled now, but he hadn't fully covered the phone with his hand. Carmen heard it all.

"I was setting up some jumps."

"Inside? We have a yard!"

"I couldn't find anything to make the jumps with in the yard."

In the kitchen Kate didn't seem happy about the doughnuts anymore. "I feel like the bottom of a trash can. Eww-eagh! I shouldn't have had those marshmallows. I felt okay when I woke up, kind of buzzy. But now… Ohhh, where's the pain medication? Carmen? Ohhh…yuck, I feel disgusting. That doughnut…"

"We have a mountain of discarded kitchen cabinets out there, Ryan," Jack said to his son in the background.

"I didn't think you'd want me to use those. They have nails sticking up."

"Okay, okay, good point about the nails, but, Ryan, you're making jumps in the house?"

"Pony jumps."

"Look, you've chipped a whole chunk out of the plaster, knocking that thing down. You can't make pony jumps in the house, okay? In a bit, we'll go find stuff in the yard that's safe for you to use." The muffled sound quality disappeared. "I'm sorry, Carmen," he said into the phone.

"Are the new cabinets okay?"

"They're fine. He didn't hit them. I was apologizing for the distraction, not the damage." He took an audible, struggling breath.

Yeah, Jack, I'm having that problem, too.

"I'm actually trying to ask you out for tomorrow night," he said.

"Oh, right. Tomorrow night?" She wanted to say yes.

Parts of her did. Large parts. The parts that had tingled when he'd kissed her, the hot skin and the soft knees. But the rest of her, the sensible, tired, emotionally stretched, surrogate-parent part…

She had Kate; he had Ryan. She'd had enough of family complications over the past few years. She would be insane to risk taking this any further.

In the background she heard Kate groaning. "Oh, hell, I'm going to throw up…" And it didn't sound as if she would make it as far as the bathroom.

"Terri is picking up Ryan at six, tomorrow," Jack said. "There's something I have to talk to her about. A whole puppy issue. It's— I don't know why I'm telling you."

"You're going to get a puppy?" Carmen struggled to follow his explanation, while thinking, Kate, how much did you drink last night that the hangover is only just kicking in now?

"No, no. I mean, not tomorrow, if we do get one. Sorry, this is just confusing things more. I guess she and I may have to talk for a while about the dog problem before she leaves with Ryan. That's why I'm telling you. So it'd be around seven before I could get to you, to pick you up. But if you don't like the idea of a Sunday night, we could leave it until Friday or Saturday next week."

"No! No, wait a minute!"

"No, you don't like the idea of Sunday, or—"

"I mean, I don't think the timing makes much difference." She took a deep breath. "I don't think I can do this, Jack. My life is too complicated. So is yours, from the sound of it. I loved it yesterday when you ki—"

"Carmen?" came Kate's frail, shaky voice. "Oh, yuck… Can you get me some water? And a towel."

"I have to go, Jack."

"Carmen, wait—"

"I just think the timing is too wrong for this."

"Right." He sounded tight, now. "It's not you, it's me. Isn't that how the line goes?" The humor was soft at the edges, gentle, but still a little forced.

"Ca-armen, are you the-ere?"

"It's both of us," she said to Jack, starting back through the kitchen to where Kate stood miserably in the hallway. "Our lives." Oh, hell, she didn't have time or space to sound tactful, or discreet, or anything. She just wanted him to know the truth. "It really is," she repeated. "This is not a line, Jack. I loved kissing you yesterday. I loved—"

"Oh, shoot, you are talking about kissing some guy, while I'm— Please get some water, Carmie? I am dying, here."

"It's not just a line." She went to the sink, took a clean glass from the draining basket, filled it with a jet of tap water.

"Sounds like you have a lot going on at your end."

"Yes. Yes, I do."

"Tap water?" Kate moaned.

"Listen, um… Yeah," Jack said. "The cabinets are going in Monday."

"Um, yes," Carmen answered.

"Okay, well, I'll see you then."

"Yes. Bye." She pressed a button to end the call, then

turned to her sister. "Yes, it's tap water. I'm sorry." She wasn't. She was angry at her sister and scared at the strength of her own feelings. "Unless you put some bottled water in the fridge to chill since I last looked?"

"No…"

"So it has to be tap water." She took a breath, aching and embarrassed, regretful and relieved, all at the same time. "Katie, please—"

"Just give me the water and get off my case, okay? I'll clean this up. So you don't have to yell."

"I'm not yelling about the mess."

I only yell at you because I'm scared, sis. And if you couldn't even notice that I just turned down a hot date with a man I really like because of you, then—

Actually, if Kate hadn't noticed, it was probably good.

Carmen and Jack took pains to avoid each other Monday, Tuesday and Wednesday morning, as they both worked on the renovation. Cormack and Rob provided useful camouflage. Tools and loud noises came in handy, also. It was hard to get personal over the scream of drills and the slam of hammers. On Tuesday Carmen went to finish the final details on another project, which made the avoidance strategy even easier.

On Wednesday afternoon, however, she and Jack once again found themselves working in the house on their own. He was painting the basement floor in a hard-wearing pale gray, while Carmen fitted the skirting boards to the base of the new cabinets.

Commendably busy and industrious, both of them.

Meanwhile, the elephant in the room that they hadn't talked about since Saturday, over the phone...

...just sat there.

Growing.

At around five o'clock Jack came up from the basement and announced, "First coat's finished."

Carmen put down her piece of board and asked without thinking, "Can I take a look?" She loved the before-and-after impressions in any renovation project, and hadn't considered *before* she spoke that *after* they went down there, she and Jack would have to stand side by side on the last step of a narrow set of basement stairs in order to take a good look.

"Sure," he answered, "if you don't mind the smell."

"I won't breathe."

I won't be *able* to breathe....

He followed her down the stairs, the first time they'd been down there together since Friday evening. At the bottom, as expected, he warned her, "That's about as far as you can go. Next bit's still wet."

They stood looking at the shiny gray expanse of concrete floor in silence. Jack had one palm pressed high against the wall and the other hand shoved into the back pocket of his jeans. Carmen could see him in her peripheral vision—the rugged line of his leg and hip and side, the backward jut of his elbow. She could almost feel his breathing, could so easily let herself sway against him and feel his chest like a warm wall against her back.

How come she could barely even see him from the corner of her eye, and yet she still had such an exact sense of the way he stood, as if they were roped together and she could feel every tiny pull? How come she could barely remember her reasons for saying no to him over the phone on Saturday, when they'd seemed so clear-cut and sensible and right?

"It looks great," she told him quickly. "It's so much cleaner and brighter. Makes the ceiling look higher, somehow. You could set it up as a workshop or a play space for Ryan. Or, hey, if you get that puppy, he could have his bed down here in winter."

"Terri and I talked. He's not getting a puppy any-time soon."

"Oh, I bet he's disappointed."

"He is."

"That's too bad. Pets are good for kids, I think."

No reply for a moment, then, out of the blue, *not* in the tone of a man discussing renovations and basements, or puppies and kids, "Why did you say no, Carmen?"

Oh, shoot.

"Saturday," he added, as if she might have misunder-stood. "Over the phone."

"I know when you mean, I know what you're talking about." Her voice came out husky. "Okay, Jack? I know. I…I was thinking about it, too."

He made a frustrated, disgusted sound. "I shouldn't push this, should I? You did say no. Like my ex and her husband saying no to the puppy. Done deal. End of story."

"No, no, it's not the end of the story."

And I'm nothing like your ex.

Helplessly, she turned to him and saw the way he was

watching her, his gray eyes narrowed and his mouth soft and still.

"If you think that what I said on Saturday was an excuse…" she said. "It wasn't. It was the truth. How can we do this? How can we follow where this might lead, when we have so much else going on? My sister is a mess, and I'm the only one there to pick up the pieces. You've just started on this new thing with Ryan coming to you five nights out of fourteen. He's the most important part of your life, and your ex is going to jump on the slightest excuse to downgrade the arrangement, from what I saw. And maybe we don't know each other very well yet, but I know enough to understand how much that would hurt you. The timing is so, so wrong. How can we?"

She put her hand on his chest, intending it as a defensive gesture, wanting to push him away. He was standing too close, making this so hard for her. She could smell the clean maleness of him, feel his body heat, see every detail in the shape of his body beneath his clothing.

But the push turned into a caress. The inch of light friction and movement between his shirt fabric and her skin felt so intimate, the first soft notes in a whole symphony of touch.

"Because we want to," he said. "You want to as much as I do. That counts, Carmen. That matters. There's your sister, and there's Ryan, but this matters, too. It *matters*."

She'd betrayed way too much. She could feel his new confidence. It was there in the way he spoke, and in the way he looked down at her. Oh, hell, he knew she wouldn't push him away now. Helpless about it, she touched his neck with the backs of her fingers while he reached out to hold her.

"Yes," she said hazily. "Yes, I guess it does."

He groaned as he pulled her against him, running his hand up her back. "I knew I couldn't be wrong about this," he whispered into her hair. She felt the heat of his breath. "On the phone you had your sister in the background. I had Ryan. But no one else is here right now. It's just the two of us. I can't get you out of my head, Carmen."

"No. I know. Me, too," she whispered.

"I dreamed about you. Do you know what your legs do to me in those work shorts you wear? Do you know how good you look in those clingy red tees? I love the way you wear earrings when you have a hammer in your hand." His arms tightened on her body and she felt shaky, the need filling her body like sugar in her blood, sweet and dizzy all over. "I planed the edge off Ryan's bedroom door on Sunday, and the wood shavings smelled like you. Hell, that is the worst compliment I have ever given a woman in my life—'Darlin', you smell like wood'— but it's true and it's good. I stood there, with the plane in my hand and my eyes shut, thinking about you and the smell of your skin, all the things we said to each other when we were working, wanting you so much."

"Me, too. All weekend. I was so snappy with Kate and Cormack."

"Monday I could barely stand to be in the same room with you."

"I know."

"Tuesday you weren't even here and it killed me. I thought maybe you'd done it deliberately, because you really did want to keep the distance. Today, all morning, I wanted to talk to you but there was never a damned moment. I caught you looking at me a couple of times."

"Oh… Yes, I…I did. You're right. I was." Not as careful about it as she'd thought, apparently.

"But this afternoon you went at those skirting boards like you wanted to get 'em done and head for the hills. I lost my nerve. It's hard, sometimes, what a man has to do."

"You like it when a woman does the asking?"

"No. I like to do the asking." His voice dropped to a growl. "But it sure feels good when I get the answer I want."

"I…I don't think I'm giving you the answer you want."

"Your body is. Your eyes are. And your mouth. Right now, I don't give a damn about the family complications."

He pressed his cheek against hers, kissed the corner of her mouth. She made a weak, pathetic attempt at turning away, but he wasn't having it. "No" she heard him mutter. "No, Carmen." His mouth closed over hers, confident and strong. He tasted perfect, felt so right. She didn't know why, didn't understand it at all, but there it was.

He felt right, and she couldn't fight this. Not now.

She let her lips part, let her body sigh against him. Recognizing his victory, he deepened the kiss, cupped her jaw in his hand, then ran his fingers down her neck and back into her hair. She gripped his backside through the soft denim fabric of his jeans and heard him groan.

The hard evidence of his need pushed against her, and she felt possessive about it.

Yes, I did that. It's for me. It's mine.

"I want you so much," he whispered.

"Mmm…yes, yes." She tightened her arms around him, felt him flinch and remembered his injury. "Oh, I hurt you!"

"It's healed on the outside but it's still tender. Don't hold me too tight, that's all." He kissed her neck and whispered in her ear, "Hold me close, but not tight. Hold me anywhere else you want."

"Let me look at it."

"I'm fine." He was still kissing her, bending to make a hot trail along the line of her collarbone.

She crooked her arm to anchor his head in place and said, "Stop. Please let me look."

"I think you just want to look at my chest." He pulled at his old T-shirt and lifted it up for her, grinning, then took it off and hung it on the stair rail.

"Well, yes, there's that…" she muttered.

Because his chest was spectacular, wide and tanned and hard with muscle. There were two scars, the neat, puckered circle where the bullet had entered and the incision line where the surgeons had had to cut into him to repair the internal damage. Both scars had fully healed now, but they still looked red and raised against the rest of his skin. She ran the tips of her fingers over the small circle, emotional about it.

He'd been shot.

*Shot!*

By an out-of-control crazy with no aim, in half darkness.

What if the bullet had gone an inch or two the other way, into his heart?

"I'm fine, Carmen, seriously."

"Oh, Jack…"

*I would never have met you.*

She didn't say it, but the awareness colored the way she touched him, the way she took his face between her hands and kissed him as if the world was going to end in half an hour. She almost forced his lips apart, made his tongue dance with hers, forgot to breathe, didn't need to breathe. "Hey…" he murmured. "Hey. Are you crying?"

"A little bit."

"How come, sweetheart?"

"No reason. Life. Fate. Those scars."

"That's too intense, isn't it?"

"I know. I was thinking about what would have happened if that bullet had gone—"

"Stop." He pressed the backs of his fingers against her lips. "Don't even say it."

"You'd better kiss me some more."

"Well, I want to, but not if it makes you cry."

"Kiss me. I don't know what it is about your basement, Jack Davey. Just kiss me."

He found her mouth again, held her close, slid his thigh between her legs. She leaned on him, hot and giddy with wanting, ready to kiss him and stay in his arms forever. Her breasts pressed into him, aching, and he cupped her with one hand and ran his thumb over the nipple that jutted hard against her bra and the soft cotton of her shirt.

"Take it off," he muttered.

He meant the bra.

"I want to touch you." He reached to her back, beneath her shirt, and unclipped the fastening, so that when she took off the T-shirt, the bra came, too. Gaze locked with hers, he balled both pieces of clothing together and threw them to the top of the stairs, where they landed just inside the open kitchen door.

Then he touched her. One nipple, then the other. Lightly. Just a brush of his fingers, and a caress that cupped each soft, rounded weight. One breast, then the other, then back to the first.

Carmen couldn't move or speak. She watched his face, then watched his hands on her skin, making every inch of her body throb. He bent his head and ran his tongue over each peak, leaving them wet and tingling. She pressed them into his face, gasping with her need for more. He sucked hard and she began to shake, her breathing frayed at the edges.

"Come to bed…" he murmured roughly. "I want you right now. Carmen, I'm dying for you, feel me."

"Yes. Yes. I know," she gasped out. "I'm dying for you, too."

Her cell phone rang.

"Don't get that." He wrapped her in his arms again,

lifted her against him. He was trembling, too. "Please!"

"I won't." She laid her head on his shoulder, dizzy and on fire.

"Let's go upstairs."

"Yes."

The phone kept ringing but finally stopped.

At the top of the basement stairs he pulled her close and kissed her again, his skin like hot satin against her bare breasts, the light pattern of hair on his chest silky and just a little rough. She ran her hands over his back and shoulders, wanting to learn their shape and texture by heart, thinking she could never get enough, wanting his mouth on her nipples once more.

Her cell phone started up again, and Jack swore.

"I'll have to get this," she told him, her voice strained.

"No. Why?"

"Because it'll be Kate. She's happy to text her friends back and forth for hours, but with me, if she wants to talk to me, she'll just keep hitting redial every two minutes until I pick up."

"I thought you were her sister."

"I am." Carmen looked at him blankly, while the phone repeated its nagging melody.

"Because you sound more like her servant."

Carmen shut her eyes. "Just let me get this. Then I'll explain." She grabbed the phone from where it rested on top of the new kitchen bench, and saw her sister's number on the caller ID, as she'd expected. "Hi, Katie. What's up?" She felt uncomfortable talking topless on the phone, and held her forearm protectively across her breasts. They felt cold now.

"What's up with you, don't you mean?" Kate said. "You're not here, and neither is Cormack, and I forgot my key."

Silently, Jack bent to the floor and picked up Carmen's T-shirt and bra. He held them out, a blob of stretchy red in one hand, and a sliver of black lace in the other.

"So you're at home?" Carmen shook her head at the black lace. She'd never get it back on, talking on the phone. She accepted the red blob.

"Sitting in the driveway," Kate said. "How come you're so late? Are you on your way, at least? I'm hungry and I can't get into the house."

"No, I'm not on my way." She got the T-shirt over her head and onto one arm, then switched the phone to her other ear.

"So, when? You sound weird. Where are you? What are you doing?"

"Kate, I can't instantly jump in the car and drive twenty minutes home every time you forget your key." She put her other arm through the T-shirt sleeve, then Jack stepped close and pulled it down her body. His knuckles grazed her sides and brought out goose bumps all over her skin. Without a bra beneath, the T-shirt fabric provided a poor barrier against the teasing brush of his hands over her breasts.

Carmen frowned at him and shook her head.

*I can't do this. Not now. I'm sorry. My sister's shattered the mood.*

"I only forgot it because you were yelling a grocery list at me as I ran out of the house," Kate complained.

"Well, you could do some shopping, occasionally. If there's no milk in the refrigerator, use a little initiative. I haven't had time to—"

"Oh, this again! Lecture Number 305, You Need to Contribute More. Hang on, who's this?" There was a pause. "Forget it, here's Cormack now."

"Katie—"

"You can deliver Lecture Number 306, the Selfishness of Kate Forgetting Her Key, when you get home, okay?" she drawled, dripping with sarcasm. "I'll have my legal pad and pencil ready for taking notes, like the eager little student you want me to be." She cut the call without giving Carmen a chance to reply.

She took the phone away from her ear and glared at it, as if it was Kate herself. "You are such a complete brat, sometimes, Kathleen O'Brien, such a complete and total brat."

"I don't think she heard that," Cormack said.

He was leaning against the front of a new kitchen counter, with his hands propped on the countertop behind him, watching her closely. The kitchen looked fabulous, Carmen thought. The glass-fronted cabinets, the blue-gray granite countertops, the stainless steel sinks, refinished hardwood flooring and brand-new appliances. They should be cooking a gourmet meal in it, not finding themselves torn between making love and downloading family problems.

"No," she said. "She didn't hear. I didn't intend that

she should. She'd already cut the call. She's an intelli-
gent brat, too, she flays me with these clever little lines
right before she hangs up on me. I hate it."

"Why do you take it? Who raised her this way, to be
so inconsiderate? How come this falls to you?"

"Because Cormack deals with it even worse than I
do, so he goes out a lot. *Opts* out I sometimes think,
although he says that's not what he's doing."

"But—"

"You want to know about my parents," she guessed.

"Do you have some?"

"No," she told him bluntly. "Not anymore."

He thought about this for a moment. "I'm sorry to
hear that. It makes a difference."

"It does, and there's a whole— There's years of
history behind it, it's not a three-line explanation. You're
right. She's rude and unpleasant, and maybe it's my
fault, but shoot, I'm only ten years older than she is. I'm
not old enough to be her mom. I signed on for this
because I had no choice. *We* had no choice, Cormack
and I. We were the eldest, and there was no one else.
I'm sorry, this isn't making much sense."

"Not yet."

They looked at each other, across the brand-new, unfinished expanse of kitchen, wry and wary. "We don't
know anything about each other, do we, Jack? I haven't
told you any of this in a proper way."

"So start. Because I want to hear it."

"This wasn't, um, what we were doing."

He ran his eyes up and down her body, where the thin

cotton of her T-shirt did little to hide the swollen shape of her breasts. Her mouth still tingled under the imprint of his kiss, and she could taste him in her mouth, smell him on her skin.

"Is the phone going to ring again, right in the middle of what we were doing, when Kate finds out you didn't get milk or frozen pizzas?" he asked.

"Probably," Carmen admitted.

They looked at each other again. He was still shirtless, his body held a little tight after the interruption of Kate's call. The scars on his torso looked fresh and sore and Carmen realized she'd probably hurt him more than he let on, when she'd held him and run her hands over his chest. Between his wounded body and her sister, how were they going to get back to where they wanted to be?

"Toss me the phone," he said.

"You're going to call my sister and yell at her?"

"No, I'm going to order us a couple of pizzas. After that, I'll turn off your phone. Then I'm going to crack open some beer, or maybe some wine, and we're going to sit and eat and talk. If that works for you."

She nodded slowly. "I'm in no hurry to get home."

"And despite the evidence a couple of minutes ago, Carmen, I'm in no hurry to get you to bed."

"No?"

"I can wait an hour. Maybe even two. While you tell me why at twenty-eight years old, working hard with your brother to run a business in a challenging industry, you're the one who gets the teen stuff from your bratty baby sister."

## Chapter Five

"Eat before you talk," Jack ordered her, a half hour later.

They sat on the chestnut-colored leather couch in his living room with a litter of cushions spilling onto the floor, music playing in the background and the smell of fresh pizza and hot cardboard filling the air. He'd opened them each a light beer and dropped a handful of napkins onto the coffee table in front of them. No plates or utensils. Just fingers.

Carmen took a slice of pizza. Strands of cheese stretched out, and she had to loop them in her fingers and pile them on top of the slice. She took a bite and tasted salt and spice and grilled mushroom. Jack tipped the neck of the beer bottle into his mouth and watched her, seeming to approve of the slick of oil on her mouth and the way she licked her fingers after several bites. Her body began to sizzle with awareness once again.

But she knew he was waiting for what she had to say, knew that this was important for both of them. If they didn't understand each other's family issues, pizza and beer and the best sex of their lives would be just another failed date.

"Mom died of breast cancer when I was fourteen years old," she started. "Cormack was sixteen, Melanie and Joe were ten and eight, Kate was only four."

Jack nodded, not taking his eyes from her face.

"My dad couldn't handle it. Couldn't handle losing her, couldn't handle taking care of us. He started drinking, just gave up, basically. I used to have to nag him to take me to the store so we could get groceries, and I'd have to say to him, watch for that truck on the corner, look out for the boy on his bicycle. Cormack used to fill in permission forms for school or sport and fake Dad's signature because he was half-passed-out and couldn't hold a pen. A lot of the time, he was too drunk to get in the car, but he got in it anyhow, even when Cormack tried to stop him." She shook her head. "You don't need this detail. About a year after Mom died, his car slid off a bridge in the rain when he was driving with a blood alcohol level five times the legal limit. And I am still so angry with him. And when Kate gets bratty I'm even angrier."

"Even though you don't want to be," Jack said. He hunched forward and took another slice of pizza from the box on the coffee table.

"No," Carmen said. "Because who does it help? Not me, not the other kids. But I can't seem to get rid of it. It's just sitting there inside me, waiting for some big moment of release that's probably never going to come."

"Same as I feel about my ex sometimes."

"Yes, and that's hard, too, but at least she's—" She stopped. How did you even say it?

"Alive?"

She closed her eyes and nodded. "With Dad, he's not. So there's nowhere for it to go. Just nowhere. No hope of ever letting it out."

She felt Jack's arm fall around her shoulder. He didn't speak, which was good, because she didn't need pop psychology from him, no matter how much he genuinely cared.

"I hum along fine most of the time," she said. "Then I have a bad day with Kate, or there are bills we struggle to pay and I am just so angry with Dad for abandoning us the way he did, for taking such risks with his own safety and well-being when we had no one else. For not listening to us, time and time again, when we begged him not to get behind the wheel. He should have been stronger. He should have been more responsible. How could he do it to Mom's memory? How would she feel—how does she feel, if she's up there somewhere and knows—about him just letting go of the great, safe, loving upbringing she'd given us up until that point?"

"She was a good mom, huh?"

"She was a great mom!" Carmen swallowed around her tight throat. "I guess that's why Dad found it so hard… Maybe I'm wrong to be angry. That kills me, too—that maybe my anger is wrong. But he forced a level of strength and responsibility on the rest of us that he couldn't manage to come up with himself, and he was the adult and we were the kids, and I'm angry. Hey, if there's a violin handy, you could start playing it about now." She laughed. "Here's another Carmen O'Brien revelation. I *hate* the fact that my life is such a tear-jerker of a story, Jack."

"You're not telling it that way. You sound pretty strong when you talk about it."

"Good! I don't always feel strong."

"Does anyone? But you can't have managed totally on your own after your dad died…"

"No, we didn't. At first no one would take all five of us. There was no money. Dad had gotten behind on the mortgage that year, so when the house was sold, almost nothing was left. Mom's brother and Dad's sister both said, "Oh, we'll take Kate." She was little and cute. But they wouldn't have anyone else."

"You didn't want to get split up between different families, anyhow, I'm guessing."

"No, we didn't. We really clung together. And no other relatives even offered that much—to take one or two of us. The only family that would have us, all of us, were an elderly aunt and uncle of mom's, Aunt Millie and Uncle Don. They were so good. 'Of course we'll have all the kids!' So we went to them and they were wonderful and they loved us and they tried. But they'd never taken care of kids before. They'd had none of their own. And suddenly they had five, and they were too old, and it was too much for them. So Cormack and I had to take a fair bit of the load even from the start. A few years later, Aunt Millie and Uncle Don died, within a few months of each other. They were both well into their seventies by then."

"Oh, hell, Carmen!"

"To be honest I think we wore them out. But they never, ever let us think that they were sorry to have taken us. Kate cried more over their deaths than she had over Mom and Dad."

"Because she was old enough to understand a little more about what she'd lost."

Carmen nodded. "So at that point I was nineteen and Cormack was twenty-one."

"Kate would have been, what, eight?"

"She'd just turned nine. Melanie was fifteen, Joe was thirteen. Aunt Millie and Uncle Don had left us their house—the place Cormack, Kate and I still live in, which was way too small when we had my aunt and uncle and all five of us there. It's okay now, nothing splashy, just a boxy pale-yellow New Jersey house with a sweet little bay window sticking out at the front and some garden in back. My aunt and uncle left a little money, too, but not enough for five kids."

"And Kate wasn't cute enough anymore, for those other relatives to want her?"

"We still didn't want to break the family up. We wanted to stay together, and somehow it was decided that Cormack and I were old enough to take care of the others. I had to quit college and go to work with Cormack. Which brings us to now, and C & C Renovations, and Kate turning into a brat, and my strategy with her is clearly all wrong, but I don't know how to do better. At least she hasn't called again."

"Yeah, because I did switch off your phone."

"Okay, do I yell at you for that or say thank you?" She made a wry face and didn't expect an answer.

"Maybe she just has to grow up, and it's going to take some time."

"That's what Cormack tells me. I get angry with him sometimes, on a bad day. He reminds me of Dad, just opting out because he can't deal with it. Maybe he's right that she has to make her own mistakes. But it seems like a risky strategy. I'm not big on unnecessary risks."

"This could be a risk that *is* necessary."

"I'll peer into my crystal ball and see if you're right," she drawled, and took another pizza slice. So did Jack.

"While you're peering," he said, "check out my son and see if he has a puppy with him."

"You're going to keep fighting that one?"

"He wants a pet. He's crazy about animals. He takes horse riding lessons. He wouldn't hurt a fly, but he'd probably hit any kid he saw being cruel to any kind of creature. He's a good kid. I don't understand why he should have to earn this." Jack frowned and fell silent.

But Carmen was thinking.

"You said he wants a pet," she said slowly, after a moment. "Does it have to be a puppy? Did your ex happen to mention kittens, for example?"

Jack looked at her. "No, she didn't. She only talked about a dog." A slow grin came out on his face like morning sunshine. "Oh, that is evil, I love it. You're right. Ryan would love a kitten almost as much. And if the kitten lives here, then it's mine, so Terri can't say a word."

He rocked back on the couch and laughed long and hard.

"Should you be enjoying this sneaky little victory quite so much?"

"Nope, shouldn't enjoy it at all." He was still grinning. "But I'm going to anyhow." He got serious suddenly. "There's only one thing I want, Carmen. I've told you already. And that's what's best for Ryan. Terri and Jay play so many games with him, and with me. I hate it, and fight it, and try to shield Ryan from it. Just this once I'm playing one, too. Thanks. I'm getting a kitten. Ryan's coming here again Monday. We'll go to the animal shelter and pick one out. I'll call them ahead of time and ask a few questions, to make sure it's going to work out."

He took a satisfied swig of his beer and stretched his shoulders, newly relaxed and content, and suddenly the awareness and heat between them flooded back. He looked at Carmen through his thick lashes and her heart began to beat faster. "That was good, wasn't it?" he said.

"The kitten decision?"

"Talking. Getting the family stuff out there, so we know what we're dealing with."

"Yeah, it was…" She noted his casual assumption that they had some kind of future together, that this was only the beginning, and her heart did one of the *clunk* maneuvers that she was getting to recognize, and the universe settled into a pleasing shape.

He slid his arm along the back of the couch, making space for her, inviting her close, and she went without hesitation. The sense of belonging was instant and overwhelming. She nestled her head against his shoulder, felt his warmth and his breathing, smelled the healthy male scent that hovered around him—soap and cotton and the tang of fresh beer.

After a few moments of silence he said, "Does it make any difference to you that I have a child?"

"Oh, please!" she said, teasing him with a smile. "No problem! Just spray a lot of air freshener around and keep him out of my sight and I'll be fine. Kind of how I'd feel if he was a pet rat. Jack, don't you think that's—?"

"It wasn't a dumb question," he cut in, way ahead of her. "You know it wasn't. Ryan comes first. He's a nonnegotiable part of my life. If you feel like you've been a parent for, what, twelve or more years already, and you don't want to have to deal with a kid being around when we see each other, that's going to make a difference. I've ended one relationship over this already, since the divorce, because I didn't ask the right questions out of the gate, and she turned out to want as little to do with my kid as she possibly could. From now on I'm asking."

And he was asking a lot.

Carmen respected his attitude. And she shared it. For both of them, there could be no such thing as a casual date. There was too much baggage on both sides.

Jack added, "Asking about your general take on the

subject, not on whether you think my boy is the cutest kid who ever lived. Just to clarify."

"I get that, Jack."

"Gotta make sure."

"If I really cared about someone," she said slowly, "I'd take on whatever I needed to take on to be a part of his life. Whether that was a child, or a disability, or the mother-in-law from hell. The *if* part is the relationship and the man himself, not the baggage."

Jack thought for a moment. Carmen waited. "What about the pet rat?" he said lightly, at last.

"I'd even take on the pet rat."

"Yeah?"

"If I could see that the pet rat was important."

"Because I haven't told you about Pinkie yet, have I? Or his little rat wifey Peaches, and their nineteen adorable babies."

"Can I just check that we're not really talking about pet rats, here?"

"Actually, I think she might be pregnant again, so make that thirty-two adorable babies."

She punched him in the arm in mock frustration, even though she knew at some level they'd traded some genuine pieces of truth about each other.

"Are we done with the soul searching now?" he asked softly.

"Well, I'm going to have to go away and think about the rat babies for at least a week…"

"It's a major commitment," he agreed, tightening his arm around her.

He rubbed his jaw against her cheek, then began to kiss her there—soft, tender kisses that spoke more, at this moment, about comfort and gratitude and trust than they did about passion. He felt safe with her and she loved that, because she felt just as safe with him.

The chaste tenderness didn't last. Soon he turned her face toward him and found her mouth. "I want you," he whispered, tasting her as he spoke. "I don't want to think or talk or stress anymore, either of us. No family problems. No adorable rat babies. Nothing. I want something that feels good…"

"Yes. I know. Yes."

"And you feel so damned good, Carmen."

"Then touch me. Kiss me."

Her words were all the invitation he needed. He groaned against her mouth, deepening the kiss with a hot, hungry tongue, pushing her down onto the slippery matte leather of the couch. He slid his thigh over hers and she felt the growing demand of his arousal and the weight of his chest.

So good, so right.

When his mouth left hers, she tried to get it back, reaching for his head with impatient hands, but then his lips began to make a hot, slow trail down her neck and she gasped. "No?" he growled at her. "Not this?"

"Yes. Keep going."

She twisted her neck and arched her back, impatient for his touch on her bare skin. He slid the T-shirt up her body and buried his face against her stomach and then between her breasts. His breath heated her sensitive skin and made her nipples peak with need. He cupped her through her bra, rolling his thumbs over her shape, a little rough about it. She loved his urgency and his single-minded maleness.

Neither of them wanted this pretty today.

They just wanted it.

Now.

"Strip, Carmen…" he said.

"Only if you do."

"Sure." He pulled back and in a few efficient movements tore off his shirt, jeans, shoes, underwear, while she fumbled at her own clothing, the heat coming and going over her body in waves.

He finished first. A good minute first. And then he just sprawled in the heap of untidy couch pillows, fished a couple more of them from the floor and watched her.

Watched her fingers moving.

Watched the wiggle of her hips.

Watched her breasts spill out of her bra and then lift higher and tighter as she reached up to take the circle of elastic out of her hair so that it fell around her face. Her awareness of his eyes raking so hungrily over her body was one of the most erotic moments of her life.

"Much better," he said.

"A man of few words."

"I can talk if you want. What do you want me to say? That I love the way you look at me with your eyes half-shut. I love that you don't have those skinny model legs with zero muscle definition. I love how big and dark your nipples are."

"Oh…"

"I love the way you smell. I want to be inside you in about three minutes and I want to hear you moaning and begging and breathing out my name. Want me to say things like that?"

"No," she said, her voice shaking. "Just show me."

"See? We don't need words…"

He reached out and pulled her on top of him, sliding her body up his chest so that her breasts grazed him from hips to collarbone. She arched her back and he held her fullness in his hands then rolled his tongue over each nipple until she gasped and sank back onto his body.

They fought the narrow width of the couch, sending the pillows tumbling back to the floor. Her arm pressed into the scar on his side and she heard him hiss with pain. "Shall we go upstairs, Jack? Would that work better? I don't want to hurt you. I want this to feel good."

He didn't answer, just pulled them both to their feet, his hands all over her so that she couldn't think straight. Or walk straight. She tripped over a pillow, knocked his not-quite-empty beer bottle over on the coffee table and then she half fell—laughing at herself—to land, elbow and palm and chest, in the puddle of spilled beer.

"Hell, Carmen…" he muttered, and pulled her wet, sticky body into his arms. "Was that my fault?"

"Totally!" But she was still laughing. "I'm fine. Not hurt. Really."

"You're sticky."

"And wet and cool and fizzy."

"I have an idea about that…" He bent his head and

cleaned the trail of beer from her stomach and between her breasts with his tongue and she had to grip his head to keep from laughing and squirming. "You're fabulous. I could lick you all over."

"We could spill some more. I'd love you to lick me."

Suddenly there was no more thought of going upstairs.

"I could lick you everywhere…" he repeated.

"Let me do it to you, too," she whispered, and bent her head to run her tongue over his skin, over the tight little nipples, the soft pattern of hair, the satiny brown skin, the tight pack of muscles between his ribs.

"Me, now," he said eventually. "My turn."

"Oh… Oh…"

He knelt on the floor in front of the couch and fulfilled his promise, running his hands and his mouth over her thighs, finding the sweet heat at her core, making her arch and writhe and beg. Just when she couldn't take any more of it, he levered his weight onto his hands, sheathed himself, and loomed over her, sliding into her while she was still whispering, "Please, Jack, please, now…"

He kissed her neck, ravished her breasts, rocked his hips. She wanted to watch him—that gorgeous male body poised over her, locked in its rhythmic waves. But after a few hard thrusts, her control shattered along with his and her eyes closed, leaving only the touch and taste of him. Giving and possession mingled together, peaking and hanging in the air before finally they lay still in each other's arms.

Breathless.

Happy.

Replete.

Traditionally, it was the man's job to fall instantly asleep, but Carmen was pretty accustomed to doing a man's job, after all. She felt drowsiness and utter satisfaction creep over her in a slow, delicious wave while Jack's body softened and relaxed and grew heavier in her arms. He was so warm. He smelled so good. The rise and fall of his breathing was like the slow swell of the ocean on a calm day.

Mmm…

Later, she had a vague, sleepy sensation of being cold, and then the slippery cotton of a puffy comforter drifted onto her bare skin. Jack had woken up, she dimly understood. He'd brought something to cover her with.

She opened her eyes and discovered him watching her, still naked. He'd done something to the lighting. This room was dark, with just a faint shaft of gold spilling into it from the adjacent dining room. In the diffuse glow, his body gleamed softly, with a patch of darker, heavier coloring at his groin.

She reached for him. "Come back. Don't get cold. Share this with me."

He'd tucked the comforter around her. She lifted it on one side and pulled him down, pressing her body against the couch back to give him enough space. They settled in together, her breasts and stomach pressed against his rounded back. She sighed, already drowsy again, although it was still early in the evening.

"If you think I'm going back to sleep…" Jack said.

"No?"

"Absolutely no."

He guided her hand down his body, and she discovered he'd spoken the truth. He had no intention of going back to sleep. They made love more slowly this time, exploring each other, talking a little. She loved the slight roughness of his work-hardened hands, and the way they could move with such intuition. He seemed to know without asking exactly where she loved to be touched, and to respond to every touch she gave him. He used protection without question or clumsiness, so that the short delay did nothing to ruin the mood.

She straddled his hips, taking control of the primal rhythm in their bodies and he held her backside in his splayed hands, teased her breasts, kissed her, pushed into her, groaned and whispered her name.

Afterward, neither of them was sleepy this time. They talked a little, then Carmen caught Jack glancing with surreptitious longing at the TV. "You want to watch football, right?" she guessed. Without waiting for his answer, she reached for the remote on the coffee table and gave it to him, grinning. "Go for it."

Jack said fervently, "You are a woman in a thousand, do you know that?" Then he gave her a narrow-eyed look. "Or am I going to pay for this later?"

"You mean am I going to say things like, 'If you don't know why I'm upset, I'm not going to tell you,' and, 'Sure, watch TV, of course I don't mind,' in a snippy voice and then withhold sex for four months?"

"Wow!" He brushed the hair back from her forehead

and looked deep into her eyes, with an awed expression on his face. "You're good! I got chills down my spine! Would you really withhold sex for four months?"

"Nah. Two minutes, tops. And only if I was really ticked off."

He laughed.

"Know what, Jack?" She stroked his shoulder, appreciating its hard, rounded shape. "I am too lazy for stuff like that. I mean, doesn't it sound like a heck of a lot of hard work to you?"

"What, getting mad and miffed?"

"Putting it into layers. Saying I'm fine in a way that tells you I'm the opposite, then refusing to explain. Having to pretend that I'm not just *pretending* to be not upset—? See? I'm already confusing myself. I am seriously too lazy for bitchiness and games and making you guess how I'm feeling. When I'm upset, you're going to hear about it. When I'm *anything,* you're going to hear about it. Loud and clear."

"And what are you right now?"

"Lazy. Ver-r-ry lazy. I wanna watch TV. And not some big drama with a ton of plot that's an effort to follow. Something easy and light. I'm thinking what would be just perfect for my current mood would be a little football…"

"Make that a woman in a million," he said. He kissed her with energetic enthusiasm, like a puppy. He clicked the remote a couple of times, then nestled back into her arms to watch ESPN.

Which was when Carmen realized that she'd lied to him, just now.

So much for the upfront and honest and non-games-playing woman-in-a-million she'd claimed to be. So much for broadcasting her emotional state as and when it happened.

Jack Davey wasn't going to hear one word about the way she was feeling right now, because suddenly it scared her. The strength of it. The intensity. The helpless happiness. The vulnerability. The unknown future and unanswered questions. The awareness of where it could lead and all the traps they could both fall into along the way.

Because right in this moment, the sweet, syrupy contentment of lying here in his arms felt way too nice and she was already in way too deep.

## Chapter Six

"This one?" Ryan said.

"Whichever one you want, buddy." At four-thirty on a Monday afternoon at the local animal shelter, Jack felt good. Generous, relaxed and at ease with the world, as only a man who's spent half of the just-completed weekend in bed with a fabulous woman can feel.

Half the weekend in bed, and most of the rest of it eating casual meals with her, planning his garden with her, watching TV sports with her, showering with her—mmm, some good memories, there!—and wandering around the hardware store. He'd never imagined that choosing paint colors, buying tools and picking out spring plants could feel like such a hot date.

Just hanging out, no games, no mixed signals, family problems put on hold, and—

Yeah.

It was good.

"I want this one," Ryan said.

He seemed so decisive about it, less than five minutes into their kitten quest, that Jack had to ask, "Why?"

"Because he's interested in us," Ryan explained seriously. "He's a people kitten. The ginger one's asleep and the long-haired one and the tabby one are interested in each other. This one likes us. We need a cat that likes us."

Indeed the nine-week-old short-haired tuxedo did seem to like Ryan and Jack. He sat at the front of his wood-shaving-filled enclosure sniffing at Ryan's hand and looking up curiously at Jack's much larger, more work-hardened fingers, which were curled around the wire struts at the top of the cage.

"I like his markings, too," Jack said.

"He's so white on his chest," Ryan agreed. "His mom must have taught him real well how to lick himself."

"Seems like we have a decision," Jack said to the woman staffing the animal shelter.

They'd spoken on the phone earlier today. "Kittens get snapped up fast," she'd warned him. "We have four right now, vet-checked and microchipped. They're healthy and real cute, but they won't last. They'll be gone in a couple of days. I'd get over here as soon as you can."

So Jack had picked Ryan up from school, along with

the backpack of gear that would tide him through until he went back to Terri on Thursday, and they'd driven directly to the shelter.

Jack took out his credit card ready to close the deal, but then Ryan pulled at his arm. "I just thought of something," he said.

"Yeah?"

"Is this the only pet I get to have?"

"You want two kittens, now?" Jack put his credit card down on the desk and the woman took it.

"No…" Ryan scrunched up his face. "But I sort of think— What happens if I— I think I want—" He stopped.

"Spit it out, Ryan."

"I think maybe I do want the pony," he announced, and seemed to think he was done.

He wasn't, because Jack had no idea what he was talking about. "What pony?" To the woman, about to process the payment for one male kitten, including feline inoculations and neutering a few months down the track, he said, "Maybe we need to hold off on this for a couple of minutes, ma'am. Something's come up."

Another family entered the animal shelter building at that moment—a mother and two blond daughters aged around five and seven. "Where are the kitties?" the younger one said. "I want a black one!"

"Jet black," said her big sister.

The little tuxedo, with his glossy black back and snowy-white chest and tummy, was the closest thing to a jet-black kitty currently in residence, and Jack felt his stress level begin to rise. Hoping for some privacy, he nudged Ryan into the adjacent room, where four generous-size pet cages currently stood empty.

"I don't know," Ryan said uncomfortably. He was totally absorbed in whatever internal dilemma had given him pause, and it hadn't occurred to him yet that his hesitation might allow the black-and-white kitten to go to someone else. "I guess I don't want it. I looked at some for sale on the Internet with Jay..."

"Ponies?"

"Yes, but I guess I like the Davey way better than the Kruger way."

"They've put the bribe up to a pony now?" Jack said, forgetting to guard his tongue. "Sheesh! I thought you were getting a puppy if you got straight As."

"The pony isn't for straight As. It's for something else." Ryan looked uncomfortable again, and Jack was bemused.

"So what's it for, bud?"

"For becoming a Kruger."

"For *what?*" He didn't understand.

In the other room, he heard one of the little girls saying, "I like the fluffy kitty and the black and white kitty."

"For becoming a Kruger instead of a Davey," Ryan explained. "For being called Ryan Kruger."

Jack's scalp tightened. "Mom and Jay want you to change your last name?"

"It's something to do with schools and, like, Harvard and stuff. Because we were late putting my name down for Jay's old school. It's a very competitive admission process." Ryan parroted the words neatly, unaware how odd they sounded, coming from the mouth of a nine-year-old boy.

He was unaware of Jack's anger, too, because Jack was currently raising his own blood pressure by at least fifty points, trying to bottle it up. "Can I just check that I have this right?" he said carefully. "Mom and Jay have told you that if you change your last name to Kruger, to give you a better chance of getting into Jay's old school, you can have a pony."

"They said it has to be my decision."

Wow. That was democratic. So thoughtful and sensible.

Shoot, Jack was so angry, he wanted to spit, and he couldn't keep it inside any longer. "Okay, forget the kitten, *I'll* get you a pony!" he almost yelled. "Then we don't have to deal with this." He knew it was rash, unwise. Knew his anger had colored his reaction, but *hell!*

"Mom said a pony would be prohibitive on your budget. Prohibitive means you couldn't afford it. There's stabling and shoeing and feed and vet bills and tack and the horse trailer. I told her you have plenty of money, cuz being a cop is an important job, but she—" Ryan stopped.

"She what?"

"I think being a cop *is* an important job," Ryan repeated stoutly, and Jack knew—just *knew*—that his son must have overheard, or directly been told, that it was a dead-end, working-class career for people with more muscle than brain, because Terri had said exactly this to Jack himself more than once.

He'd never thought she'd sink as far as saying it to

their child. What else had she been saying? Just how far would she go to strip him of his masculinity in their son's eyes? And how the hell did she and Jay dare to do this? Bribe a nine-year-old to agree to changing his name without consulting the man who'd given him that name in the first place?

He didn't know what got to him more. The shameless, mercenary nature of the bribe, the fact that Terri and Jay hadn't talked to him about this first, or the one-eyed snobbery of their assuming that Ryan had to have a rich guy's last name in order to amount to anything in the world's greatest democratic nation.

In all the mess and games and betrayal of the divorce, Jack had never been as angry as this. His head was pounding and his throat had choked up. From the other room, he heard the girls' mother say, "If we don't get one today, it might be a while before we can get back here, and even so, they still might not have a black one. I think we should get one of these. They're all adorable, don't you think?"

From somewhere inside him, he pulled out a tight little parcel of control and told Ryan, "For now we're getting the kitten, so if you're still set on Tux and not Fluffy or Carrot or Tiger we'd better tell these little girls that he's already taken, or they may be disappointed." Since the animal shelter staffer still had Jack's credit card on her desk claiming the kitten as his, he felt this was fair. But the little blond five-year-old might not see it that way and he didn't want to upset her.

"Are those really their names?" Ryan asked.

"Temporarily. But we can call him whatever you want, once we get him home."

And he was going to shelve the pony and name-change issue temporarily, too. He'd already let his son see too much of his emotion on the subject, which wasn't fair to—

Hell! Why on earth should he care a damn about being fair to Terri?

But he knew the answer to that one.

Because she was his son's mother.

And because he wouldn't sink to the level of playing those games.

"The fluffy one is sooo soft," said the older girl. "Is it a girl or a boy?"

"That one's a girl," the animal shelter lady said.

"Oh, we want the fluffy one!" said both girls, which reduced Jack's stress levels by one percentage point.

At least he wasn't going to have to deal with knock-down kitten wars today.

So they paid for Tux and took him home and set him up with a soft-sided padded kitty basket to sleep in and a little tray and a saucer of fishy food, and the little guy seemed happy to be here in Jack's half-renovated house. Both little guys seemed happy—the kitten and his new owner.

Jack, on the other hand…

He needed to vent his feelings somehow. Talk to someone. Yell his anger in safety. Spit his sense of injustice and betrayal. Find someone who'd understand, who wouldn't take Terri's side or give him a whole lot of too-easy advice or feel uncomfortable at the emotional nature of the conversation.

Which ruled out his friends, his fellow cops, his parents and his sisters.

And left Carmen O'Brien.

Of course.

Oh, Lord, he wanted to talk to her about this right now!

About twenty percent of the explosive feeling disappeared as soon as he thought of her, and ten percent more ebbed away when he picked up the phone.

All of it came back in a rush when Cormack O'Brien told him, "She's out, Jack, I'm sorry. She and Kate went to a movie, and then they were going to eat somewhere."

Which Jack knew was probably good news for harmonious relationships in the O'Brien household, but not such good news for him. Sometimes Carmen's family demands and his own were going to end up in competition with each other, he could see.

"Is it something I can help with?" Cormack finished. He'd completed his work on the kitchen refit at the end of last week, and Carmen herself would only be back for a couple of hours on Wednesday to do the final touches. The downstairs half bath had been stripped of its old tiles and fittings and awaited the arrival of the newly ordered supplies sometime in the next couple of weeks.

Very soon, if Jack wasn't seeing Carmen in a personal context, he wouldn't be seeing her at all.

"No," he said. "It's nothing."

"Shall I take a message? They only left about half an hour ago. Or you could try her cell. If they're not inside the cinema yet, she may still have it switched on."

But she didn't, and Jack was left with nowhere to go. It felt like one of the hardest evenings of his life.

Somehow he put together some pasta and salad for an evening meal, using the spacious, efficient new kitchen without an atom of pleasure. He agreed that Tux—the name had stuck—could sleep in his basket on the floor beside Ryan's bed. They watched a little TV together, Jack, his son and the cat. Ryan did his homework, and was tucked under the covers by eight-fifteen. Somehow the kitty basket now sat on his pillow rather than on the floor, but Jack didn't have it in him to protest about this tonight.

When he checked on the two of them half an hour later, they were both dead to the world. Ryan's hair looked dark and soft against the pale pillow. Tux had snuggled right up to the padded edge of his basket with his chin resting on his miniature black and white paws. The white tip of his little black tail had fallen against Ryan's cheek, and Ryan was smiling in his sleep.

They both looked so innocent, Jack thought. Neither of them deserved to be caught up in his and Terri's conflict, or her games.

A fresh wave of anger hit, and his eyes began to sting. Out of nowhere, the shooting ambushed him again—the waste of a life, the loss of a child's mother, the worst-case scenarios that seemed all too real—only this time he didn't have Carmen's arms to fall into and he couldn't even reach her on the phone.

He hauled himself up to an acceptable level of emotional control and went on the Internet instead.

For heck's sake, if Jay Kruger could make millions on the stock market… Shoot, the man could buy half a dozen Triple Crown contending Thoroughbred stallions and not even notice the dent in his bank balance, how the hell did he have the gall to mess with a nine-year-old's head over one pony this way?

"If Jay can make money on the stock market, so can I," Jack muttered to himself as he stared into the brightness of the computer screen. High finance had always struck him as the most boring, pointless thing on earth—he preferred hands-on reality, thanks—but if getting involved in it could do anything to level the playing field between himself and Jay Kruger, then maybe he should change his mind.

He still had several thousand dollars left over from his uncle's inheritance which he hadn't yet specifically earmarked for the renovations. He could open an Internet trading account right here and now. He followed a few prompts, keyed in a few details, and the thing was done. Ignoring the sense of recklessness ringing in his head, he told himself he was taking a positive step.

"You did what?" Carmen said.

They sat in a family-style Italian restaurant five minutes from her place on Thursday night, with plates of meaty, cheesy lasagna in front of them and a Caesar salad to share in the middle.

"I opened an Internet trading account," Jack repeated.

"What's that going to achieve?"

"You don't mess around with your words, do you?"

"You like that about me." She leaned across the table and stroked her index finger over the back of his hand, grinning a challenge and an apology at the same time.

He didn't argue her point, because it was true. He did like her honesty. He needed it, the way he needed her brown eyes fixed on him with such an intent, listening expression, needed her curvy figure sitting there in a clingy black top, needed the long, jet-black earrings swinging against her neck, needed everything about her. "I was just so angry," he said.

"Are you going to be good at it, do you think? I wouldn't be, I'm sure. Buying low, selling high, all of that."

"Well, it bores me to death, if that's any indication."

"Yeah, not a good one." She smiled again, but he could see the concern in her eyes and it soothed something in his soul.

He trusted her.

She cared.

"I am not the patsy, Carmen," he said. "I am not the dumb cop. He's my son. And I can see them nudging him away from me, little by little. Talking down my values. Talking down all the things I'm good at and want and care about and believe in. Putting Jay and his values in my place. Money and status and winning at all costs, instead of honesty and hard work and trust. And Ryan is nine. He doesn't really understand what's going on. I'm going to lose him if this keeps up. Lose my stake in who he is. What do I do? Do I not fight? Do I just let it all happen?"

"Fight *your* way, not theirs. Trust your son."

"What does that mean? What would you say if I gave you that sort of advice about Kate?"

She sighed. "You're right. I'd say it's not as easy as that."

"Exactly." They were both silent for a minute. Jack didn't want to talk about it anymore, not the whole share-trading idea, nor his hurt and anger about what was happening to Ryan. And to himself. He asked instead, "So how did it go with Kate on Monday night?"

"Oh, we had a good time, to start off. Laughed at the movie, enjoyed our meal. But then there was a message from Courtney when we got home, wanting Kate to go out drinking, and as soon as I pointed out that she had a breakfast shift the next morning she turned sullen, acted like I was her jailer. And I wanted to be! I wanted to lock her in her room and not let her out until she grows up. She's still nearly three years underage! You're right. It's not easy to sit back and trust. You do want to fight. Has Ryan said yes to the pony, and to changing his name?"

"He's thinking about it. He would love a pony. He's already learning to ride. I can see the battle going on inside him."

"Some kids would have said yes right away, without a second's pause for thought."

"Yeah?"

"I like him, Jack. I think you're doing a great job with him."

"Want to see him on the weekend?"

"You mean if I don't see him, that also means I don't see you?"

Jack nodded and their eyes met, and they both knew how much he was asking about the nature of their relationship with that single, outwardly simple question about seeing his son. They'd talked about it last week— that crazy conversation about pet rats. They both also knew how much she would be telling him with her reply.

"I want to see you, Jack," she said softly.

But she had to push back a sudden wash of fear and doubt at the commitment she'd just made.

Ryan had a book report due Monday and he'd forgotten to bring the book, which he was only partway through reading.

"Where is it?" Jack asked. "School?"

"Home," Ryan answered, then corrected himself quickly to add, "My other home. Mom and Jay's."

"How long's the book? Can you finish it Sunday night when you get back there?"

"It's long."

"Okay, so is it going to be a big deal if you're a couple of days late with the report? Can you tell your teacher you left the book at your mom's instead of bringing it here?"

It had to be a common enough problem—kids with complicated custody arrangements leaving their homework with the wrong parent.

Ryan looked distressed, but said manfully, "I guess."

"How many pages do you still need to read?"

"About two hundred."

"Two *hundred?* Why did you pick such a long book?"

"Because there's lots I want to say about it in the report. It's a Harry Potter book. They're always long. Even when they're too good to put down they still take a while."

"You're up to reading Harry Potter? That's great!"

"I'm up to the third one, and I've written, like, ten sentences of the report, but I left that at home, too."

Ryan actually sounded as if he wanted to do a good job on the assignment, which wasn't exactly a common occurrence. If he was treating his homework as important, for once, Jack didn't want to send a message to the contrary. He knew he was going to have to call Terri and see about getting the book and Ryan's "ten sentences", even though Carmen was due here any minute.

It would be a family-style occasion, just for the afternoon and evening. She would leave tonight before Ryan—and his kitty—went to bed. She and Jack had agreed that she wouldn't stay over when Ryan was here. Not yet, was the unspoken afterthought. Not for a while. Not until they knew more about where this was going. The issue of what was appropriate for his son made an already complicated situation even more so.

As did Terri's response to Jack's call. "I have errands to run this afternoon. I'll drop the book over to you."

"What time, about?"

"Do I really have to be specific, Jack? We're not talking about confidential corporate account statements.

It's a book and a piece of paper with kid writing on it. No one's going to steal it if you're not in and I end up leaving it on the back porch."

He swallowed the back-handed barb about the corporate account statements—Terri's implication that she and Jay dealt with such things on a day-to-day basis, and that they were important, and that Jack was so thick he couldn't prioritize between company secrets and a child's school work. "Sure, leave it on the back porch," he said in a neutral tone. "I'm not sure what we're doing this afternoon."

"It wouldn't hurt if you planned ahead. Something constructive for him, like a cultural event or a nature walk, instead of lounging in front of TV."

Well, see, that's where you and I are different, Terri. Because I think kids can produce cultural events and nature walks in their own backyard if you just turn 'em loose, and who in the hell mentioned TV? Not me!

He didn't say it.


Carmen brought lunch to Jack's—fresh crusty bread, deli meats and salads, chilled blackcurrant and apple juice, a half-size bottle of champagne and some mini fruit tarts for dessert. They could eat picnic-style in the backyard. She knew Ryan would be here, and it was a gorgeous early-May day. Tux was going to be given his first chance at exploring outside, under close supervision. She and Jack probably didn't need such close supervision from Ryan, themselves…

At the front door, Jack met her with the phone in his

hand, but he must have finished his call because he didn't say anything about it, just pulled her into his arms for one of those lusty, lip-smacking kisses of his that made her laugh and heat up at the same time. His strong muscles tightened around her, his gray eyes sparked across the space between them like an electric arc welder, and his grin told her he was looking forward to this as much as she was.

A picnic in a big, messy, western New Jersey backyard, in company with a kitten and a nine-year-old?

Yeah, crazy, but the whole thought of it made her heart go light and her body start singing.

"What did you bring?" he asked, looking at the grocery bags she'd put down on the old floor.

"I'll set it out on the picnic blanket, and then you'll see."

"Don't have to use a picnic blanket. I bought some outdoor furniture this morning at a garage sale. Really solid, good quality. Could do with sanding and re-staining at some point, but I've cleaned it off and it looks good."

She ran her fingers down his cheek in a saucy caress. "Maybe I'd rather use the blanket."

"You would?"

"Get horizontal. Get a little sleepy after the champagne, while Ryan plays with Tux. Might have to lay my head on something soft, like your shoulder."

"Mmm, you brought champagne."

"Just a half-size bottle. I felt…fizzy."

He kissed her more softly, taking his time, brushing his lips over her mouth. "Fizzy is good."

"Fizzy is very good. Kate's almost been pleasant over the past couple of days. And did I convince you about the picnic blanket?"

"You did."

Ryan was hungry already. Carmen set everything out and the three of them ate without much conversation. Predictably, the nine-year-old finished first. "Can I bring Tux out now?" he asked his dad.

"Remember what we talked about, though? Don't lose sight of him. He's only ten weeks old. Take it slow."

"I will. He goes through the whole house now. He's not scared." Ryan disappeared inside and Jack used the opportunity to lean across and kiss the champagne taste from Carmen's mouth.

"You're right," he said. "We only had a glass each, but it's making me sleepy out here in the sun."

"Too sleepy to kiss me?"

"Never too sleepy for that…"

Ryan returned after only a minute or two, with Tux held carefully in his arms. He set the kitten down on the grass and Tux sniffed around and caught sight of a dead leaf stirring in the breeze. He pounced on it, a ferocious hunter capturing his prey. He rolled onto his back, held the leaf with his front paws and kicked it violently with the unsheathed claws on his back legs.

*You're toast, leaf.*

Ryan giggled and found more such challenging creatures for Tux to chase. Twigs. Wisps of grass. Tux was the king of the jungle.

After ten or so minutes, kitten and kid both got bored.

"Can I take him some other places?" Ryan asked. "Show him the whole yard, and round to the side, and the trees?"

"Sure, as long as you keep watching him," Jack said. "He can move pretty fast when he gets going. Don't take him too near the freight line embankment, because he could easily get lost up in all that undergrowth, and he'd be hard to reach."

"I'll keep watching him," Ryan promised.

Kid and kitten disappeared around the far side of the house.

"My secret plan has worked," Jack said.

"Yeah?"

"I'd rather kiss you in private. Kittens can be such voyeurs."

But the privacy only lasted a minute. Carmen heard the sound of a car engine and recognized Terri's vehicle in the driveway. Did Jack's ex have a built-in radar? This was the second time in just a few weeks that she'd interrupted something like this.

Jack groaned, rolled over and scrambled to his feet. "This will be Ryan's book report that he left behind at Terri and Jay's. She said she'd drop it in during the afternoon." He loped toward the car, as if he wanted to head Terri off before she saw that he had someone here.

Too late.

Terri had already stepped out of the car, covered several yards of grass toward them, and looked past her ex-husband's shoulder to discover the kitchen remodeler lying on a plaid blanket amongst a telltale scattering of picnic remains. "Where's our son?" she asked through a tight mouth.

"Playing at the side of the house with Tux." Jack pressed his lips together as soon as he'd finished the last word, and Carmen could tell he hadn't meant to say it.

Except that it didn't matter, because it turned out Terri already knew about the kitten.

"Right," she said. "Tux. I've heard about nothing but that damned animal all week." She stopped abruptly and lowered her voice, but Carmen could still hear every word. She busied herself tidying up the picnic things, hating to be caught in the middle of this, for Jack's sake and Ryan's. If she could have disappeared into the house without being too obvious about it, she would have done so.

"You did this to sway his decision on the pony, didn't you?" Terri said.

"No, I did it because I didn't think he should have to 'earn' a dog. I didn't know about the pony when we went to get the kitten. The pony is really low, Terri, a real low blow."

"I...I don't know what you mean." For once she looked and sounded flustered—guilty and caught off guard.

"Did Ryan get it wrong, then? Sounded like a pretty straightforward transaction to me. If he agrees to become Ryan Kruger instead of Ryan Davey, he gets a pony. Isn't that how it's going to work?"

"It's not as simple as that. For heaven's sake! It's a complicated issue. And maybe you could tell me why your kitchen person is—"

"My kitchen person is Carmen. A friend. Girlfriend, if you want. And I don't think lifelong celibacy on my part was a condition of the new arrangement with Ryan. Now explain the complication."

"It's— I don't expect you to understand how these things work, Jack."

"Because I haven't had the benefit of Jay's lectures on the subject? Or because I didn't get a classy enough education?"

Terri closed her eyes, then bravely opened them again and stared Jack down. "Ryan needs to get accepted into the right school, and you have no idea how competitive it can be."

"You and I didn't go to the right school. We went to Lincoln High. And I cycled there every day until the start of twelfth grade."

"Yes, and look at you now."

"Look at me now. Fixing a house I love. Doing a job I'm proud of. Spending as much time as I can with Ryan. Happy, Terri."

"Scraping by. Closing off our son's future options every day like slamming doors in his face because you're proud of your blue-collar life."

"Of course I'm proud of my life. It's good and decent, and if it's not glamorous, so what?"

"Well, I want something better for him. Is that wrong? I want him to have the chance to *be* someone. To have influence and success."

"Whereas I want him to have decent values, and those values include family pride, and if you're really so ashamed of the Davey name, Terri, I'm amazed you managed to carry it for so long."

"I was young and naive, and so were you."

"Not so naive, in your case. You managed to land a rich boss and get him to put a wedding ring on your finger."

She sniffed. "You and I had separated before Jay and I became involved."

"Yeah. Before. You're right. What? A whole week before? You think your technical failure to commit actual adultery lets you off the hook? I don't."

"Let's stop this."

"Good idea."

"And let's not get caught up in all the ways we don't see eye to eye. The breakdown of our marriage is in the past, Jack. Move on! As Jay and I have said to Ryan, the name change is totally his decision and we're not putting on any pressure."

Hmm. A pony wasn't pressure? Carmen wondered. She watched Jack struggling for control and felt a flood of emotion and relief when he won his battle and swallowed his angry reply. He didn't need to be a part of this, descend to Terri's level. He was worth more than that.

Terri, leave Ryan's homework with his dad and go, she wanted to say. This is *his* weekend, not yours.

"Dad! Dad! Tux, no! No!" All three of them heard Ryan's voice at that moment, cutting across the unresolved tension just as Terri began to walk toward the car. He was yelling, his tone urgent, and his voice carried clearly from the far side of the house.

Carmen scrambled to her feet. Jack's feet thudded on the ground as he broke into a sprint.

"Tux, don't!" they heard Ryan say. "Come back! I can't reach you now!"

"Oh, mercy, what's happened!" Terri gasped in Jack's wake, and began to run, skittering in her heeled sandals. "Jack, if you've let him—" She didn't finish, just let the angry half threat hang in the air.

## Chapter Seven

Ryan appeared around the corner, meeting Jack seconds later. "Tux went up a tree," he said, sounding agitated and distressed. "He's gone too high and I can't get him and he doesn't want to come down. I didn't think he'd go up that fast."

"Which tree?"

"The big one."

"The pine tree?"

"Yes."

Ryan led the way, and the three adults reached the base of the big old tree and looked up. And up. And up. Apparently, this kitten could climb.

Apparently he couldn't climb *down*.

Still scrambling wildly, with his little claws digging

deep into the soft pine bark, he reached a narrow side branch about fifty feet up, clawed his way onto it, then stood there with his little white-tipped tail quivering against the trunk of the tree as he began to meow with a piteous sound and a wide-open pink mouth.

Ryan called to him hopefully. "Tu-ux. Tuxxy… Here, boy. Just turn around and climb back down. Just stick your claws in and come down."

But Tux didn't budge.

"Call the fire department," Terri said. She began to search in her purse for her cell, to make the call herself.

"I'm not bothering those guys for something like this," Jack growled at her.

"Oh, right, because they're heroes with way more important things to do."

"They are."

"Like sitting around in their uniforms playing cards and polishing their damned pole." Terri's disparagement wordlessly put firemen and cops into the same basket and tossed both groups aside…even while she wanted one group's help. Carmen wasn't impressed. "I'm calling them," Terri repeated.

"Don't," Jack said. "He'll be down by the time they get here."

She put her hands on her hips and tilted her expensively styled blond head to one side. "How, Jack?"

"Because I'm going up there myself."

"I'll help with the ladder," Carmen offered quietly. She knew where it was, and that it wouldn't reach all the way up, but it would help.

Jack shook his head. "Just as easy to climb the trunk."

Carmen saw that he was right. Starting at around four feet from the ground, the tree had horizontal branches at irregular intervals like the treads of some bizarrely constructed set of stairs. Jack might get a little scratched on the way up, but he'd be safe. He didn't waste any time about it, found his first foothold at almost chest height and hoisted himself up, his arm muscles knotting below the sleeves of his T-shirt and the denim of his jeans tightening across his butt.

"Tux'll be down in three minutes, Ryan," he said, as he began to climb.

"How will you carry him, Dad?"

"I'll tuck him into my shirt and knot it at the bottom so he can't fall out."

He looked good—strong and confident and athletic. A man to believe in. A man to trust.

Actually, Carmen admitted to herself, he looked like the sexiest man she'd ever seen. Trying not to grin too openly with sheer appreciation, she let her gaze rove over his body as he climbed—the tight, hard pecs and abs and biceps, the ropy forearms, the powerful movements.

But Terri only watched him with her hands still on her hips as if waiting for him to royally screw up so she could tell him "I told you so!" Carmen saw that she still had her cell phone in her hand, visibly itching for the moment when she could dial 911 after Jack's mission failed.

Ryan hopped from one foot to the other, impatient but with no doubts. He believed in his dad and trusted him, too. "Yay, Dad, go. Tuxxy, Dad's coming for you, okay? You don't need to get scared."

The kitten was already scared.

He'd scrambled up there in a blaze of feline overconfidence, joyfully discovering the skill in his little paws, but now he didn't have a clue what to do next, and the ground must look an awful long way down from that height when you were that small.

Oh, oh, wait, no! What was he doing now?

"Tuxxy don't go down the branch," Ryan called.

But Tux wasn't listening. He began to ease himself along the branch, putting one tiny, nervous paw in front of the other until he was two feet away from the trunk, then three feet. The branch started to get thinner. Much thinner. Any minute now, the kitten's weight would begin to make it bend.

"Shoot," Jack muttered, looking up. He still had probably twenty feet to go, despite how skillfully he'd picked his hand- and footholds on the irregular pattern of branches, and how quickly and strongly he'd climbed.

"I am calling 911," Terri declared, talking more to herself than to Jack or Ryan or Carmen. "I will not be a party to this insanity any longer." She rounded on Carmen suddenly. "I guess he's doing this to impress you. Pathetic, isn't it? Or are you the type who *is* impressed by this level of immaturity and Neanderthal skill?" Her words carried. Ryan must have heard them, and so did Jack. Carmen could see it in the way his movements had gone tight.

"I don't think he's doing it to impress me," she said quietly.

Terri smiled, a somewhat forced expression. "Oh, you don't? Then why?"

"In defense of innocence? For Tux because he's scared. For Ryan because he loves his pet."

Terri looked impatient at this. "And does that kind of thing put dinner on the table?"

"Are you saying Jack used to have you going hungry?"

"I'm not speaking literally, of course. I'm making a point. Take it or leave it."

Carmen left it.

Jack had ignored the exchange and reached the kitten. Or at least, he'd reached the branch.

The kitten was now a good five feet from the main trunk, and the branch had begun to bend. His little tail was quivering again and he'd frozen in place. Jack stretched his arm across but couldn't reach. He looked down at his feet, checking the size and strength of the branch he stood on, and Carmen could see what was in his mind. He was going to edge his way out along it until he could stretch up and sideways to grab that tiny bundle of black and white.

She yelled up at him before she even knew she was going to speak, "No, Jack!"

She caught a tiny glance of malicious satisfaction from Terri, but didn't care about the other woman's moral victory. She only cared about Jack—staying safe, taking no risks, listening to her fear.

"Can you get him, Dad?" Ryan called out, his trust still absolute.

"Yes, I'm going out to him now," Jack called back.

Terri had her cell phone up to her ear.

"No, Jack!" Carmen repeated. "The branch won't hold your weight that far out from the trunk. You'll have to stop. You have to come back to the trunk. Now!" The branch had already begun to bend.

"I'm fine."

And that was when Carmen lost it. That was when the flashbacks flooded in, along with the helpless anger that she had no power to negate or control or argue away.

*I'm fine.*

She'd heard those words too many times before, spoken recklessly and without pause, just the way Jack was speaking them now. Spoken by her father without a thought as to his own safety or the consequences to the people he was supposed to care about and protect, if he turned out to be wrong—if he wasn't *fine* at all.

"Don't, Jack," she said. "I'm asking you…telling you, don't."

She didn't yell. Just said it, cold and hard. Her veins had turned to ice, her emotions so powerful that she couldn't even name them. Anger. Fear. Dread of her own reaction as much as anything else. If he went along that branch, would her growing feelings for him change forever? Would she ever feel safe again?

"Seriously, I'm fine," he repeated.

"You're not fine," she said. "The branch is too thin. Don't try it. Terri's right." She turned to Jacks' ex. "Are you calling?"

Terri didn't answer directly. "Fire department, please," she said into the phone. She looked up as she spoke. Carmen followed her gaze. Jack was still edging his way out along the branch. He'd taken no notice of Carmen's protest at all.

And then the branch cracked. Loud, like a gunshot.

"Dad!" Ryan yelled.

The branch gave way, broken at a point two feet out from the trunk. Just in time, Jack grabbed the kitten with one hand while the other gripped the branch above his head. His legs dangled in the air, while the branch he'd been standing on angled uselessly a foot below his reach. He was going to fall. Carmen felt ill. Anger and fear made an acid cocktail inside her and she couldn't move or even speak.

He should not be doing this.

He was the father of a child who needed him, loved him, depended on him.

He should not treat his own safety so lightly. Not when he had better options. *Any* options.

She just waited, watching it happen, wanting to run and run and run until she forgot she'd ever known a man named Jack Davey. With sickening clarity, she saw her own father's car plow through the bridge rail, playing like a movie in her head. She knew what it would have looked like because some unthinking family friend had driven them over that same bridge on an errand the following day before the gap in the railing had been fixed—the black-and-yellow police tape had still been in place—so the image that haunted her had always been incredibly vivid and real, loaded with her anger and grief.

With equal clarity she saw Jack hammering and

thudding and scraping from branch to branch as he fell, his body tearing on a hundred jagged pieces of wood and bark along the way, his limbs floppy and unmoving when he landed head-first on the hard ground.

She saw it before it even happened.

And then it *didn't* happen, because miraculously he hung on with that one hand until his foot found and just anchored itself to the stronger, unbroken section of branch closer to the trunk.

He hadn't fallen.

Yet.

"Yes, the address is..." Carmen heard Terri say into the phone.

But he wasn't safe yet, either.

His body was strung between the upper and lower branches at a sharp, agonizing angle, almost fully stretched. After his recent injury and surgery, the pain must be killing him, *must* be weakening his hold. How was he going to get himself straight, get a strong enough grip with his feet to be able to maneuver his upper body back toward the trunk?

"Dad! Dad!" Ryan kept shouting.

Still at that terrible angle and working with one hand, Jack managed to pull the kitten against his chest. He attempted to shove the little creature down the front of his T-shirt, fighting Tux's instinctive struggle. "Don't, Tux, don't," he said. "I'm trying to help you, little guy."

Finally Jack won that particular battle. His right arm, clutching the upper branch and supporting probably seventy percent of his weight, had begun to tremble with effort. But now, how could he let the kitten go? The shirt wouldn't hold Tux in place on its own if the kitten didn't have the sense to cling to the fabric.

Carmen watched, still frozen.

"Can you wait just a minute?" Terri said to the emergency dispatcher.

Jack twisted the hem of the shirt into a kind of knot and shoved it tight and deep into the waistband of his jeans. Carmen could see that Tux had his claws unsheathed in terror and was clinging directly to the skin of Jack's chest as hard as he could, but the man gave no sign that he was in pain, either from this or from his gunshot injury. He let the kitten go—it stayed safe in his shirt—and pulled his freed hand out from the shirt's stretchy neckline.

"O-kay, there we go," he said easily.

But Carmen could see that his whole body was wired tight and shaking. He gripped the upper branch with both hands at last and worked himself upright again, a few feet from the trunk. Seeing that he was vertical and that his body wasn't tortured by its painful stretch, Carmen could at least breathe a little better.

He eased his feet and hands back along the upper and lower branches until he reached the comparative safety of the trunk, where he paused and took a couple of heaving, shaky breaths. "Nooo problems, Ry," he said.

If his son was fooled by the casual tone, Carmen wasn't. He'd come so close to falling. So close. Had he damaged his injured chest?

"Never mind," Terri said tersely into the phone. "The situation is in hand. We don't need anyone after all."

Within two minutes Jack had reached the ground. His forehead and neck were beaded with sweat, his skin was clammy white and his lips were dry, but he was grinning as he reached into his shirt neck for the kitten.

"Yay, Dad! Yay, Dad! That was so cool!" Ryan hopped up and down again, grinning too. "Tuxxy, are you okay? Can I have him, Dad?"

"Well, you could, only I think he's nailed himself permanently to my chest in about twenty different places." He looked at Carmen, still grinning, wanting her joking response.

She shook her head and closed her eyes. She couldn't treat any of this as an adventure, or as a joke. She could still hear her dad's voice. *I'm fine.* Could still see that torn gap in the bridge railing and the ghost of her dad's car spinning through it to the water below.

"This has been fun, Jack, as usual," Terri drawled, "but I need to go. Ryan, sweetheart, I'll see you tomorrow night, okay?"

"Okay, Mom."

"I'm so glad your kitty is safe, honey."

Carmen opened her eyes in time to see them hug each other quickly, Terri's face reflecting her powerful and almost ruthless love for her son. "You'll have your book report done?" she asked, frowning at him a little.

"Yeah, maybe."

"Need to earn those A grades. Jack?" She appealed crisply to her ex. "Make sure?" She began to walk in the direction of her car.

"If I survive the attack of the killer kitty claws." He'd begun to coax the kitten to let go. He threw another look at Carmen, wary and thoughtful now. He could see she was…

What? Angry? Close to tears?

Some strength flowed back into her legs, but she felt totally at sea.

What next? Stay? Spend the rest of the afternoon with him the way they'd planned? *Swallow* this?

Or bail now.

While she still could.

"You were great, Dad," Ryan said. "I almost thought you were going to fall."

"Yeah, there was a suspenseful moment or two," Jack drawled. He'd calmed the kitten down enough to pry the claws from his chest. "Hey, better take Tux inside, I think. He's had a scare, too. Want to play with him in your room for a while, then see if he'll go to sleep in his basket?"

"Do cats have adrenaline?" Ryan asked. He took the kitten tenderly in his arms and began to stroke him behind his little ears.

"If they do, he's used up a year's worth this afternoon," Jack said. "And a couple of his nine lives."

"Tuxxy, let's go see if you need a nap." Ryan and the kitten disappeared around the corner to the back of the house.

Jack turned to Carmen and spoke slowly, studying her. "You look as if you have something to say."

"Don't ever, ever do that again."

"Climb a tree? Aww, come on! It's too much fun!"

She wasn't ready to laugh. Not one bit. And Jack knew it, she could tell. "Do not ever, ever ignore someone telling you you're not safe, when it's someone who cares about you." Her voice cracked. "And someone who does not want to have to watch you killing yourself, risking your life. And when your son is watching. Just don't. Don't—*do not*—say *'I'm fine'* when you haven't even thought about the risks and you're not fine at all."

"You think I would have gotten seriously hurt, if I hadn't got a hold of that branch? Carmen, there was a lot of stuff to catch me on the way down. I would have been scratched to pieces but not broken."

"That's not the point."

"Then what's the point? You don't trust my risk-assessment capability?"

"The point is—I've said what the point is. Don't brush off someone's concern for your safety. Don't take your own life lightly when you have a child to protect. Don't show off, or play the hero, or try to prove something to your ex or whatever you were doing up in that tree just now. *'I'm fine.'* You were not fine. I have been through this before. *'I'm fine.'* While my heart is in my mouth. While I want to cry with fear. While my future and the future of people I care about—innocent kids— is hanging by a thread. And I am not prepared to go through it again. Ever. For anyone."

Saying it out loud gave her the answer she needed. On legs that felt half-numb, she turned and headed for the house. Her purse was inside. Her sunglasses. The picnic supplies she'd brought…? They could stay. A parting gift for Ryan and Jack.

Because she couldn't do this.

She expected to hear Jack coming after her, but there was no second slam of the back screen door once she'd walked through the house herself, picked up her purse and sunglasses from the front hall table and reached the front door. In the car, she couldn't get the key into the ignition for a good thirty seconds, her fingers were like rubber. She still expected to see Jack appearing around the side of the house or on the front porch, ready to beg her to stay.

But when she'd finally started the engine, strapped herself in, taken a couple of deep breaths and decided she felt safe enough to turn from the patch of grass where she'd parked and head down the driveway, he still hadn't appeared. Only as she waited for a passing car before turning into the street did she see him, standing motionless in the front doorway, watching her go.

He didn't call, didn't come down the steps, didn't wave.

Which was probably good.

She knew he had Ryan with him until Sunday evening, and he was a good father. She wouldn't see him again this weekend, even if he did care enough to push this. He wouldn't let his own personal problems get in the way of one of these new, precious weekends with his son.

She was on her own, with only the memories of her dad's death to keep her company.

As it turned out, Carmen had her baby sister to deal with, to distract her from thinking about Dad and Jack.

Kate didn't come home Saturday night, which meant that neither Carmen nor Cormack slept.

Carmen met her big brother in the kitchen at four in the morning, raiding the refrigerator. "This is insane!" he said. "I'm thirty-one years old. I am not supposed to have to wait up listening for an out-of-control teen coming home. I do not want to be here, Carmen! For damn sure I am never having kids of my own."

"Leave that window open, Cormack. Don't say *never.* One day you might meet—" What on earth was she doing? Thinking about herself and Jack and even a future family, when surely their relationship was over?

But Cormack was implacable. "No. No way. I've done it already." His anger veered abruptly into concern. "Do you think she's okay?"

Carmen shrugged a your-guess-is-as-good-as-mine response.

"Sorry. It was a dumb question," he said.

"I'm not going to call hospitals yet."

"Go back to sleep. Let me eat cold pizza in peace."

"You're not sharing?"

"Want some?"

Carmen took a piece in silence and went to eat it in bed.

The next morning at ten, when Kate still hadn't shown or called, she started contacting her baby sister's friends. But none of them knew where she was. "Have you tried her cell?" they all suggested helpfully, which made her want to scream.

Oh. Gee. What a good idea. I never would have thought of it.

Because Kate's cell had been switched off without interruption since four o'clock yesterday afternoon, and Carmen knew this because she'd called it more times than she could count.

At noon, Cormack began calling hospitals and the New Jersey police. Carmen thought about Jack. Thanks to his insider status, might he have some shortcut to the whole process? Know of some emergency database he could try on their behalf?

But after the way she'd left him yesterday, she couldn't call him now, just because she needed help.

"Is she…" Carmen found it hard to say the word to her brother out loud. "…*missing,* at this point?"

"Whoever I talked to doesn't seem to think so. If they were fobbing me off because they have more serious stuff going on, I don't know. She's eighteen. She can vote and drive and pay taxes. She's probably with some new guy."

"You say that like it's *not* one of the scariest scenarios of all, given some of the guys out there, and given Kate's nonexistent capacity for good judgment right now."

"Everyone has to make their own mis—"

"Don't say it, Cormack!"

"—stakes. Boy, you are edgy today."

Yeah.

She'd put on one of her favorite weekend skirt-and-top outfits this morning, had washed her hair, put music on in the background, tried her hardest not to panic about Kate's absence, or to fret over her angry departure from Jack's yesterday, but none of it had helped.

And by eight in the evening, there was still no word from Kate.

When the doorbell sounded at ten after the hour, it was Jack, not their baby sister.

He leaned into the door frame, gray eyes narrowed and wary. Clearly, he didn't know if Carmen was going to let him in. Neither did she.

"Could we talk, at least?" he asked quietly. He wore his usual casual clothing—aged, snug-fitting denim, a dark-blue polo shirt, a lightweight jacket in the New York Giants away-game colors of red and white.

"Ryan's gone back to his mom?" She didn't move to let him pass, so they both just stood there. Carmen's tense hands wanted to smooth down her stretchy top or pick at the side seams of her flowing skirt.

"I drove here as soon as they left," Jack said.

"Did he get the book report done?"

"Most of it. Enough to keep Terri happy."

"And how's Tux?"

"I think he's licked all my dead skin cells out from under his claws by now. He's fine. Ryan thinks I'm a hero," he added, with a flicker of something in his eyes. Defensiveness?

"If that's supposed to be an argument in favor of what you did—"

"You were talking about your dad, weren't you," he cut in, "with that *'I'm fine'* stuff."

"I was talking about you."

"You're saying this because of your dad," he insisted. "Carmen, it's not the same. How can you think I'd let Ryan down by not taking care of myself? I barely drink. I—"

"It's the same to me."

"I'm a cop. Are you saying I have to give that up, too, if I want to keep seeing you? It's not exactly the safest career on the planet."

"Of course I'm not saying that."

"So what's the difference?" He stepped closer, hunching his shoulders.

"Some risks are worth taking. Some risks have to be taken. I can deal with that. I could. I think. The world needs heroes. It does. It doesn't need irresponsible fools. And I definitely don't! Ryan is wrong to think you're a hero for going after that cat the way you did."

"I'm not a fool, Carmen. Hell, you're starting to sound like Terri."

She pressed her lips together. Yeah, it was an unlikely alliance, herself and Jack's ex. "Okay," she said.

"Okay, what?"

"Okay, if I sound like Terri, then I'll have to just sound like Terri. I'm not going to back down on this. I cannot deal with you playing the hero to prove yourself to your son. It's different from what Dad did, but it adds up to the same thing. Pointless, thoughtless risks. Weakness, not strength. I cannot deal with it."

They looked at each other.

"So what are you saying?" Jack asked slowly. "Hey… you're shaking."

"Yes."

He came closer, reached out for her, and so help her, she didn't push him away. "Carmen…"

"I don't know what I'm saying."

"Know what I'm scared you're saying?" he whispered. "That you really don't want to see me anymore. Don't say that. Don't."

He began to kiss her. Her neck. Her hair. The corner of her mouth. As soon as their lips met, she wanted the whole of him. The way he smelled and tasted, the way he groaned out her name when they made love. Helplessly she parted her lips and gave him her heart through their kiss. He touched her lightly, almost questioningly, brushing the tips of his fingers down her arms, resting his palms on her shoulders, taking her hands in his, cupping her jaw. He didn't speak, but she knew what he was asking with every touch.

Stay in my life.

Just stay.

Please stay, so we can work this out.

With a shudder of surrender, she tore her mouth away from his and fell harder against him, wrapped her arms around his neck and put her head on his shoulder. He felt so strong and warm, and every instinct told her to feel safe with him. Could she trust those instincts? She didn't know.

"I guess I overreacted a little," she finally said, not knowing if it was true.

"And I shouldn't have gone so far out on that branch. You're right. It was an unnecessary risk, and I'll stop to think for longer next time."

"Please. Even if you think I'm crazy."

"I kind of like you crazy."

"Oh, Jack…"

"Have we dealt with this?"

"I…I think so." But she couldn't be sure. She sensed that it had been too easy, that they'd both conceded and apologized too soon, because they were looking for the right excuse. They wanted each other so much, and that hadn't changed.

"Can I come in?"

"Kate's missing," she blurted out.

"Wh— Shoot, seriously missing? Hell, Carmen, why didn't you say?"

"I don't know if it's serious. Maybe we're overreacting, Cormack and I. I don't trust my own judgment today."

"Because of me and Tux and the tree."

She nodded. "Cormack's gone to a movie. Said he couldn't stand hanging around the house hoping she'd show up or call. I can't be mad at him for it, he wanted me to go, too, and I know he barely slept."

"Tell me. From the beginning." Jack led her inside and she went instinctively toward the kitchen—the place she'd last seen Kate, pouring herself coffee at eleven the previous morning.

"No one seems to have seen her since yesterday before noon. I said goodbye to her when I went to buy the things for our picnic. When I got back… When was that?"

"After the kitten? Around three, if you came straight here."

"…she wasn't around. No message. I tried her cell at around four, but it was switched off and has been ever since. Cormack and I both lay awake listening for her, but she didn't show, and her friends are either playing dumb—which in itself does not reassure me—or they really don't know. He called hospitals and the police this morning."

"She's eighteen. You have no reason to be concerned for her safety."

"Other than the fact that she *is* eighteen. And wild. And too pretty. And her decisions haven't been good ones lately."

"So no one's taking you seriously, yet."

"No."

"They see this kind of thing all the time."

"I know. But this is my sister."

"Hey…" He touched her gently. Her shoulder. Her cheek. "I'm on your side. Let me make some calls. Wanna put on a pot of coffee?"

"You wouldn't prefer a beer?"

"I'll have coffee," he repeated in a neutral voice. A little too neutral. It gave Carmen a jolt of fear. Did he expect to be up late? *What* did he expect? She hated to think about some of the things he must have seen in his work.

He took the cordless phone into the living room while she found coffee filters, filled the jug, opened the can of aromatic grounds. She heard snatches of what he was saying. "Yeah, hi, Danny, it's Jack…" There was a clipped authority in his tone that she hadn't heard before, a confidence that somehow seeped its way into her own bones and made her feel just a little better. "Bleached-blond, shoulder-length, I haven't met her, I'm going from a photo… No… Yeah, maybe some… Okay, thanks."

There was a lot more that Carmen didn't catch and didn't try to, because she was too scared. It seemed to be a long conversation, or else he'd been transferred to a couple of different people. She heard him repeat the physical description, using blunt, standard phrasing that dehumanized Kate, although she knew it wasn't Jack's fault. The description made her shiver. Bleached blonde, five foot eight, average build. It made Kate sound like a corpse. Sometimes TV crime shows had a lot to answer for.

She's eighteen, ran the mantra in her head. She's grown up. She's *selfish*. If she even understood that I worry about her like this, she'd think it was my problem, not hers. She's not going to rush to let me know she's okay. She probably hasn't spared me a thought.

Finally, when the coffee had dripped through and filled the glass jug, Jack came back into the kitchen. "No reports matching her description," he said. "I need some more details from you, then I'll call a couple of other people."

"Details?"

"On her associates."

"Associates?" She could only parrot his keywords back at him.

"Guys, in particular," he explained, incredibly patient with her slowness. "New guys, and especially anyone she's mentioned by name whose background you don't know. We can run them through our system and see if we come up with any kind of a record. Drug dealing, anything."

Carmen felt ill. "Then you do think something's happened."

"I think you're worried sick about her and I'll do anything I can to help. Want to pour me that coffee, while I write down some of these names?"

But Carmen didn't have many names. Kate had been so secretive lately, pushing her bossy older sister away whenever she tried to find out about Kate's life, her friends, anyone she might be seeing. If Kate had a new boyfriend, Carmen and Cormack would be the last people to know.

"Who does she confide in?" Jack asked. "Who does she really talk to?"

"Melanie, our other sister—we both talk to Mel better than we talk to each other—but she's in Chicago, in college."

"We'll call her later, after I've checked on these other names."

Taking absentminded gulps of the hot, milky coffee, he made another long call while Carmen slumped on the couch and listened, taking in only the broad gist of his inquiries. Kate's previous loser of a boyfriend had a drug conviction, which didn't surprise her.

The names of her female friends didn't show up in any database. Carmen hadn't been able to tell Jack the last names of several people, male and female, whom Kate had mentioned in passing.

"Do you keep a message pad beside the phone?"

"Yes, but there was nothing on it from Kate. Didn't I say?"

"Do you keep old messages you've written down for her?"

"That message pad is months old!"

"So you might have some names and numbers there."

He was so good. Just so efficient and calm. Talking her through the possibilities. Knowing who to call. Getting his fellow cops to take this seriously in a way that Cormack hadn't been able to do, hours ago. Thinking of things—leads on finding Kate—that wouldn't have occurred to Carmen on her own. Making her believe, just by the way he handled everything, that Kate was going to be fine.

"Thank you, Jack," she said to him when he'd finished.

"I'm sorry there's nothing. But the statistics in a situation like this are so much in her favor. She'll be okay. Ninety-nine times out of a hundred, they're okay. All I can do is keep telling you that."

"You've done more than I could have. You're here. That's enough."

It was a kind of apology for the way she'd reacted to the tree branch incident, and he must have known it. He sat down beside her on the couch, put his arm around her and pulled her against him so that her head could rest on his shoulder. "Where else would I want to be?" he said softly.

She turned her face to him, wanting his kiss, wanting to taste him and touch him and feel again how *right* they always were together. He brushed her jaw with his fingers, parted his lips and nuzzled her, printing kiss after kiss on her mouth, her closed lids, her neck, and back to her mouth again. She melted. Everything melted.

The impatient hammering on the door roughly ten minutes later made them both jump and swear. Carmen scrambled off the couch and went to answer it, pulling her top down and smoothing her mussed-up hair.

Kate stood there, bedraggled and tight-faced and miserable.

## Chapter Eight

"What happened to you, Katie? Sheesh! Where have you been? Why didn't you call?"

Kate didn't answer, just pushed past Carmen so she could get into the house. Her shoulders were hunched and tight, and her hair hung over her face like a screen.

"Something happened," Carmen repeated.

Kate skulked into the living room, saw Jack and stopped in her tracks. "Oh, jeez, you have company."

"So come upstairs and talk to me there."

She hugged her arms around her body. "I'll tell you here. It's no great drama. My purse got stolen, that's all. With my cell phone in it, if you're wondering how come I didn't call."

"When? Why didn't you—"

"In the night, I guess. Or this morning." Her control and bravado began to falter. "I was…yeah…with friends."

"Where?"

"Some horrible place. I don't know where it was."

"That doesn't explain—"

Kate cut in angrily, "I know it doesn't explain, okay? I know I shouldn't have gone there." Her control and hostility broke suddenly, along with her voice. She needed to talk, Carmen saw, and she didn't need an interrogation.

"What can I make for you?" she asked gently. "Something to eat? Hot chocolate?"

"Would you, Carmie?" Kate's voice trembled a little. "I need a shower. Like now. It was a crack house, or something. I don't even think there was a refrigerator let alone a land line. It was so filthy. I was too wasted last night to notice." She bit her lip and stopped, blinking back tears. "And—and then scrambled eggs on toast, with the hot chocolate? Could you do that? I haven't eaten since last night. Or I guess yesterday lunch, really, if you're talking actual food."

"Bacon and grilled tomato and hash browns on the side?"

"Yes. Please. All of that. Could you?"

"Of course I could."

"Thanks…" She disappeared upstairs.

"Jack?" Carmen turned to him.

"We can report the purse."

"Is it just the purse? She looked—"

"Something's shaken her up, given her a scare." He

stood up. He'd deliberately kept a low profile, just now, staying on the couch while Carmen and Kate talked. "Let me go cook while you find her some clean pajamas or something. Deal with her physical needs, take care of her a little, don't keep hitting her with questions. That's the best way to get the story from her."

He ran his hand down Carmen's back, and she just wanted to hug him and cry and say thank-you for being here, thank you for being *you*. "The bacon is in the—" she began.

"Shh, I'll find everything. Don't worry. Just go up. If she's in the right state to open up, you want to catch it while it lasts."

"How do you know all this?"

He shrugged. "I'm a cop. We see this stuff."

"What stuff? What do you think happened?"

"I don't know. Lots of possibilities. Go find out."

Carmen found fresh pajamas for Kate in a basket of clean laundry on the landing at the top of the stairs. While her sister was in the shower, she had time to put fresh sheets on the bed and light one of the scented candles Kate used to perfume her room. She didn't dare straighten up the room, although it could certainly use it. She'd gotten a hostile reaction to such attempts before.

Kate was fragile enough to be grateful for her sister's cosseting. She came out of the bathroom, wrapped in the huge, fluffy clean towel that Carmen had slipped through the door. She gave an exclamation of delight when she saw the bed.

"Clean sheets? Oh, that's so good!" She gave Carmen a hug. "I was so stupid," she said.

Carmen bit back another demand for details. "But you're here now, and clean, and safe, and smell that bacon downstairs?"

"Will it burn?"

"Jack's doing the cooking." She waited.

"I woke up. I had no idea what time it was. Midafternoon, probably. I was on a mattress on the floor. There was a guy lying on it with me. Carmie, I don't know his name. I don't even know if…if I slept with him. I had my underwear and my top on, but—"

She stopped, and once again Carmen forced herself to wait. No questions. No yelling. The smell of hot food drifted stronger and stronger up the stairs. She'd barely eaten, herself, tonight. Worrying about Kate had taken her appetite away.

"And then I couldn't find my purse. It had my cell phone in it. Looking for it was so horrible, combing through every room and finding, must have been six or eight people lying around, off their faces. Made me see just how disgusting the place was. Otherwise I might not have, you know, seen the detail. But the purse wasn't there. Everyone else was still passed out, and I didn't recognize any of them. I had no money. I found some quarters in a jar and took them. I just left. But then I had no idea where that place was. I couldn't remember how I'd gotten there. I thought it was Newark, but it turned out to be Union City. I got all turned around."

"Why didn't you find someplace to call from?"

"I couldn't find one single phone booth that wasn't trashed. One of them ate three of my quarters without putting a call through, and I thought what if I leave myself without enough for a bus?"

"A cab? You know I would have paid for it at this end."

"It was a horrible neighborhood, Carmen, and I looked like a wreck. I didn't think anyone would pick me up, not that any cabs went by, anyhow. I felt like I was stranded in a foreign country. I…I guess I was still a little wasted, I wandered around, it seemed like hours. I couldn't come up with a plan. When I saw Manhattan across the river at one point, it was so weird, because where I was just felt like…yeah, I said this…a foreign country. I took the wrong bus, I should have waited for one that went to the Port Authority." She plastered on a tight smile. "Anyhow, I'm here. I…I just wish I knew if I had sex with that guy."

Carmen hugged her, stroked her hair. "Do you feel as if you did?"

Kate shook her head, still uneasy. "My clothes weren't messed up. I hate not knowing for sure. That's the thing I hate the most. Go away now, Carmie, let me get dressed."

Carmen went downstairs, more emotional than she wanted Kate to see.

In the kitchen, Jack was serving food onto two plates. "Thought you might like some, too," he said, and she just nodded and lowered herself weakly into a chair. It all smelled so good. "How is she?" he asked.

"I don't think she'd want me to give details. There

are a couple of things bothering her. It's not as bad as it could have been. Do you mind if I don't say any more?"

"Just as long as you think she's going to be okay."

Kate appeared a few minutes later, and she and Carmen ate together without talking much. "Oh, this is so good!" Kate said a couple of times, and she looked around for Jack as if wanting to thank him.

But he had gone into the living room with his cell phone, and Carmen guessed he was probably following up on the calls he'd made earlier, telling his contacts that the missing "bleached blonde, five foot eight" was home safe.

She felt another huge rush of thankfulness that he'd been here. If she'd stayed angry with him and sent him away… If something worse had happened to Kate and she'd had to deal with it on her own…

"Want some more hot chocolate?" she said to Kate, flooded with all sorts of emotions she couldn't put into words. "Another piece of toast? Shall we put on a DVD?"

"You're not going somewhere with Jack tonight?"

Carmen laughed and teased her, "Oh, yeah, like I'm leaving you here on your own."

"Well, that's what I want, actually. Seriously, don't stay on my account." The sudden shift from needy to hostile was typical. "You are sitting there watching me like I'm a bug in a jar."

Carmen swallowed a sigh. There was to be no miracle transformation of attitude resulting from Kate's scare, it seemed. "Jack probably needs to get home," she said.

"I'm hoping he'll invite you along," Kate drawled.

"Listen, Katie, I've been thinking. Shall I call the doctor and make an—"

"Stop, okay? No more heart-to-hearts. No helpful advice. No offers. I seriously want to be left alone now, Carmie." On a blast of sarcasm, she added, "To contemplate my foolish behavior and make massive life changes because I've seen the error of my ways. Will that help?"

"I am not leaving you alone tonight. Oh, and by the way, if we're doing anger and sarcasm now, even though I am almost crying with relief that you're home and safe, I am so angry with you for giving us such a scare, and for taking the risks that you do. If you want to know."

"Thanks for the news flash, sis." Kate picked up her empty plate, and Carmen's, and took them both to the sink to rinse them. "I'll call Alicia and see if she can stay over," she said over her shoulder. She opened the dishwasher. Then she turned and appealed to Jack, who'd finished his calls and returned to the kitchen. "Take her away? Please? For the night? So I can have some peace?"

"She cares about you, Kate, that's all," he said gently.

"Yeah, well, I appreciate her care in the abstract, but it's actually not all that helpful right now. I'm thinking a vodka and orange might be more what I need. Or six. And a little bourbon to chase them down."

Jack threw Carmen a look which said he understood her frustration. "Coming?" he muttered. "Wanna just… come to my place?"

She nodded in silence, then added, "When Kate's called Alicia." She didn't really think that Kate intended to get drunk tonight, but seriously did believe she shouldn't be alone. And she was happy to hear Alicia's name, rather than Courtney's. Alicia was at least a little more grounded.

They heard Cormack's car in the drive just then. Kate stepped to the window to check that it was him, then grinned with evil triumph at Carmen. "Satisfied now? Cormack'll be here to hide the booze and the cash from naughty Kate. And he won't try to *talk!*"

"This is a first, do you realize?" Carmen said to Jack at his place half an hour later.

"Yeah?" He could see a wicked little twinkle in her eye and wondered what was coming next.

"I brought a toothbrush."

"A new toothbrush?"

"Yep. Bought it the other day."

"And you're planning to leave it here?"

"Yep."

"Wow," he said. "Commitment."

"I know. Scary. How many adorable rat babies am I going to be sharing your space with?"

"Are you scared, Carmen?"

Oh, hell! Dammit! She was.

Jack could see it in her face as soon as he asked, and cursed himself for letting the words slip out as if they were nothing more than a joke. They looked at each other, and he just wanted to touch her, make love to her, lie naked with her and hold her all night long, without thinking about the future or their families or anything else.

"You don't have to be scared…" He engulfed her in a big hug, clumsy in his emotion. His first kiss aimed at her mouth but missed and he didn't care, just used the scatter-gun approach. Every inch of her felt so precious, it didn't matter where his lips made contact. She still tasted perfect, smelled perfect, felt perfect in his arms.

"I'm scared anyhow," she whispered. "Don't tell me it doesn't make sense. It makes total sense. Tell me you're scared, too."

He pulled back, intending to deny it, but then it hit him that she was right. They both had a lot to be scared about, so many ways to mess this up. He'd met her halfway on what had happened when he'd rescued Tux yesterday, and he understood the way her father's death had marked and changed her, but he didn't really know how deep it ran. Some people never got over something that scarring from their past.

"Do you want to talk about it?" he offered, feeling like a starving man offering someone else the last pizza on the planet.

*Please don't say you want to talk about it, Carmen! Just kiss me some more and then take off your clothes…*

Her clothes stayed in place.

But her hands moved to his chest. To the buttons down the front of his shirt, which she began to unfasten one by one. "We should talk about it," she said. "Please don't make me do that tonight. If there's any therapy happening, can it be this instead of talking?"

She ran her fingertips lightly over his skin and he groaned.

Yes, oh, Lord, yes!

"You're fabulous, Carmen."

"No. Just honest. And not very brave."

He thought she was probably the bravest woman he knew, going into business with her brother, raising bratty Kate, but when he tried to say so, all that came out was an unsteady breath, and the words, "Don't stop that!"

She murmured, "Tux really scratched you to pieces yesterday."

"Yeah, I would have yelled, except he would have gotten scared and just dug in deeper."

"Looks to me like he was already in about as deep as he could go." She frowned as she ran her fingers over his chest some more, her touch as light as the brush of some soft fabric. "We should put something on these," she said.

He only needed her fingers. They soothed his skin far better than any cream. He closed his eyes, his focus arrowing down to this one place in the whole universe— her fingers, his chest.

"Aren't they hurting you?" she said.

"Not now." His voice had begun to fray at the edges. Could she hear?

Oh, yes.

She could definitely hear.

This wasn't her fingers on his chest anymore. It was her lips, now. They pressed on his skin—slow, moist imprints that teased his nerve endings crazily into life. On the sore places. On the places Tux hadn't reached. Everywhere. She knew what she was doing to him. Exactly what she was doing. Her lips touched his nipple and the hot drift of her breath made it tighten and burn. She started a trail across his chest toward the other nipple and his whole body twitched with impatience.

The only part of her body touching him was her mouth. Print. Press. Taste. Just her mouth. Over and over. Almost as if she didn't want to permit herself—or him—the use of her hands. Then he felt the graze of her teeth, the lap of her tongue, a tightness as she sucked his nipple, bit on it gently, salved the brief moment of near-pain with her wet tongue.

No woman had ever touched him like this before, treating his chest as if it had the same aching sensitivity as her own breasts. It did. Oh, jeesh, shoot, it did, and he'd never known before. He didn't have words for this.

"Don't stop," he gasped out, just standing there in the middle of the room with his shirt unfastened and open at the front, his eyes closed and his body flaming.

"Have to stop," she said, her voice purring like a panther's. "Can't keep on with this forever when there's so much more to get done."

"What?" he asked stupidly.

She laughed, all husky in her throat. "Haven't made up my mind, yet, about what exactly. I'm not planning this, Jack. I'm just…exploring." She dropped her purring voice even lower. "I love that your eyes are shut. Don't open them…"

"Okay." He loved that she wanted the control and that she used it so playfully.

Now she added her hands to the mix, running them over his skin where he was already cool and wet from her mouth. He felt her pause, heard some movements and the sound of fabric and skin together. What was she doing? A moment later she slid the unbuttoned shirt down from his shoulders, turning the action into a slow caress.

When the shirt reached his wrists she reached around to grab the fabric at the back and used it to pull him against her body. He felt the push of her breasts, two full, heavy shapes that grazed his chest with deliberate intent. Feel me. Feel my peaked nipples. Feel the weight. Feel the way I'm sliding them across your body. Touch them. Feel just how full they are.

He wanted to touch them. Oh, yes.

But he couldn't. She was using his shirt like a strait-jacket, twisting it and pinning his arms inside it. He couldn't reach her with his hands. He had to chase her with his mouth. Bending, he searched for her, his mouth wet and hungry. It didn't even occur to him to open his eyes.

He found the deep valley between her breasts and kissed her there. Her breasts bounced and pushed against his face. He almost whimpered with the need to touch them, but she still had his arms tangled in the damned shirt and only his mouth was free.

Free and searching.

Finally he captured one nipple in his mouth and sucked hard, eyes still closed but remembering how those tender peaks had darkened and thrust out when-ever they'd made love, hard as pebbles. She gasped and her body whipped up and back, pulling him with her.

She dropped the shirt and he shook it free of his hands and onto the floor and then he just grabbed at her.

"You wait, Carmen. Just wait."

He cupped her breasts in his hands, tracing their swollen shape, lifting them to his mouth. He opened his eyes at last and found her standing as helpless as he'd been a moment ago, her head tipped to the side and covered by a wild curtain of hair, her mouth open to take ragged, panting breaths.

He took her in his arms and held her against him, felt the way she was trembling, and had a fierce impulse to cut this short, just get to the primal, animal point of the whole thing because every time they'd gotten there before it had felt so good and he couldn't stand to wait for it a moment longer.

She must have guessed.

Yeah, well, the way he pulled at the waistband of her skirt gave a clue or two.

She laughed and took his hands away, dropped to her knees on the rug before he could stop her. She wrapped her arms around his waist. Her mouth ran down the center of his body. To his navel. To the pads of muscle that ran between his hips. Lower. He tried to help but she wouldn't let him and her fingers moved so deftly that she'd unfastened his jeans and pulled them down, along with his underwear, while he was still trying to draw breath.

She was going to use her mouth.

His whole body tightened in anticipation and his need surged even higher as he felt the first moist touch. She circled him with a hot, wet darkness that moved back and forth, and he curled his fingers through her hair purely to anchor himself to the planet.

"You're going to have to stop that."

"Who says?"

He couldn't answer, he was so close to the edge. At the last moment he dragged her head away and pulled her back onto her feet, shaking with the effort of holding himself back.

"No?" she whispered, touching her lips to the curve between his neck and shoulder.

She still wore that damned skirt. She looked like a mermaid, with it twisted around her lower body while her bare breasts jutted from beneath the stream of dark hair that had fallen around each shoulder. He felt the skirt swishing against his throbbing shaft, and even that was enough to bring him back to the brink.

"What's in it for you?" he whispered.

"Plenty."

"What else do you want? Let me give it to you, Carmen. Whatever you want."

"Whatever *you* want. Surprise me."

He laughed. "Might surprise both of us, if you give me an open invitation like that."

"Is it good, though?" She began to kiss him, a juicy berry on his mouth, soft butterflies on his eyelids and cheekbones. "Tell me this is good for you."

"The best. The best ever…"

They looked each other full in the face, and the universe stopped and went still. He read in her eyes exactly what had surged in his own heart. This was *important!*

He'd always suspected it.

Now he knew.

This wasn't just two people meeting, connecting, waving goodbye. This was huge and real and deep and *fragile*. They'd either make it work—really work, growing-old-together work—or they'd hurt each other to the bone, scar each other for life, and the whole thing was too new for either of them to yet know which it would be.

The power of the understanding took Jack's breath away, made him feel as if he'd just had his kneecaps slammed with a tire iron. His legs were starting to buckle and he could almost have cried.

And yet there was a strength to it, too. Knowing how important this was gave him a kind of compass point to aim toward. Get it to work. Don't go down the hurting path. Put some effort into it, because you know it'll be worth it if you can get it right.

You failed once, Jack.

You and Terri.

Just wrong.

So many ways.

We were too young.

This time, don't blow it.

"The best," he repeated and held her so tight she probably couldn't breathe right, and neither could he.

The best.

Except for the damned skirt.

The way it was twisted, he couldn't find the zipper. She couldn't, either. As she searched for it, he captured those gorgeous, sexy nipples in his mouth again and they both gave up on the zipper and he just kissed her breasts and her mouth until she was arching and gasping and begging.

He'd started to think that she always begged, and he loved that. The sound of her breathing grown so out of control and that husky, impatient, pleading voice, "Oh, yes, Jack, oh, please, oh, please…"

"What? This is what you want?" he teased her.

"Don't do this…" She was laughing and gasping and whimpering and pulling on him, all at the same time.

He reached down and managed to untwist the skirt from across the front of her body. He thrust his hand between her thighs and felt how hot they were. She lifted the skirt and once again it brushed across his swollen shaft like the touch of her fingers.

Beneath the skirt, her high-cut bikini briefs offered little as a barrier. He cupped her silky-skinned backside in his hands, loving its peachy shape, its weight, the way it spread against his palms. What the hell was a red-blooded man supposed to do without curves on a woman? Without all this roundness and fullness and weight to hold in his hungry hands?

She rocked herself against him, hot and damp and swollen, totally unashamed about the way her body showed that she wanted him.

"Aw, hell, how do we always let this happen?" he groaned. "We're downstairs, and the bed is upstairs."

"What's your fixation with beds?"

"Not so much the bed. What I keep in the drawer beside the bed. We need those little packets, remember?"

She groaned, too.

Then she did a couple of deft, magical things with her hands and her hips and her thigh and somehow he was inside her, right where they stood, with that little pair of bikini panties—red ones?—simply pushed aside. "Just a little bit," she whispered. "Just one push. Please?"

Aw, hell, she was begging again.

Making magic with every fraction of an inch that her hips moved.

And she didn't know how close he was.

With a shudder, he managed to slide himself—*wrench* himself, more like—free of her hot, delicious folds.

Just in time. Or *almost* just in time.

"Upstairs," he said through clenched teeth. "Or I'm not responsible."

They made it. *Almost* made it.

She was begging again. "Please, oh, please, Jack, don't let me go, don't hold back." She almost sobbed out the words. He reached the bedside drawer. Found what they needed. She took off the mermaid skirt and the bikini briefs—yes, red—and reached for him and they got there in seconds.

Afterward, lying in her arms and listening to the total contentment and relaxation and release in the way she breathed, he felt so sure about her—about the growing old together, not the hurting each other to the bone—he fell asleep with a grin on his face and a bursting heart.

## Chapter Nine

"Carmen?"

"Yeah, Katie? What's up?"

Kate had her announcement expression in place. Carmen knew it well. It usually signaled that a request for money would be involved somewhere in the ensuing conversation. It was a Wednesday afternoon in June, several weeks after Tux had gotten stuck in a tree and Kate had gotten stuck in a crack house in Union City.

"I've been thinking."

"You wanna be careful with that," Carmen teased gently. "It can lead to actual ideas."

"Yeah, well, I've had one of those." Kate took a deep breath. "I want to go back to college."

"Think they'd have you?" Carmen was still teasing.

She didn't know if it was the right strategy, but probably better than immediately going, "What? How? Why? Have you thought this through?" in an atmosphere of enormous suspicion.

"I only have one incomplete on my transcript. And anyhow, I don't want to go back to MCC."

Maplegrove Community College.

Close.

Convenient.

Inexpensive.

Not particularly high on anyone's list of the country's best. Kate had drifted into her place there because a couple of her friends were going. She could have done better, and she'd lasted in her chosen and very light-weight program for less than a semester.

"I want to apply for somewhere like NYU or Rutgers."

"You've left it very—"

"Late. I know. If I've already missed out for the fall, maybe they have a spring admission, or I'll just have to wait a year. We'll need to do some research. I want to go back and talk to the careers counselor at the high school. She had some good ideas for me, but…yeah…I guess I didn't listen. I want to go somewhere that has a really well-regarded premed program. You see, I've decided I want to be a doctor."

"This is a little sudden, isn't it?"

Kate shrugged. "For you, maybe."

"Kate, for heaven's sake!"

She had the grace to look shamefaced. "Okay, so I've sort of been thinking about it for a couple of months. I know I made a mistake stuffing around at MCC and dropping out. And…you know…that day when I couldn't find my way home…when I had to go see a doctor to find out if I'd slept with a guy whose name I didn't even know."

"You did that? You went to the doctor? Dr. Lopez?"

"Yes, Dr. Lopez."

Lara Lopez was the family practitioner they'd gone to for years. Carmen thought she was wonderful, but she wouldn't have been surprised if Kate had skulked off to a complete stranger. Somehow, the thought of Dr. Lopez was very reassuring. She'd be a great role model if Kate was serious about a medical career.

"I couldn't stand not knowing," Kate went on. "Like if I could be pregnant or get HIV or something and not even know if there was a risk."

"You didn't tell me."

Kate shrugged. Too embarrassed, her body language said. Now she informed Carmen grudgingly, "Dr. Lopez said there was no evidence of actual intercourse. She was great."

"She is, and that's good, isn't it? The no-intercourse thing? That's what you wanted?"

"What I want is for you not to get in my face on the subject of every, like, megabyte of my existence. I don't want to mess up my life, okay? That's all you need to know. That's what you want, isn't it? For me to decide I don't want to mess up my life? I'm worth more than that. Are you going to yell at me about it, and say 'I told you so,' like, a million times?"

"Might leave that to Cormack, actually," Carmen drawled.

"Oh, Cormack won't," was Kate's offhand prediction, and she was probably right. Cormack's best strategy in the surrogate parenting department was his closed mouth.

"No, and I won't, either," Carmen promised. Although she didn't want to bring up the issue, she had to add, "But, Katie, most colleges with good premed programs cost a lot of money."

"I'll get student loans."

"That's not what I'm saying."

"So what are you saying?"

"Cormack and I will want to help you out financially, but only if you're serious about this."

"I'm serious. I'm not saying I'll breeze through it and be all sweetness and light about the whole thing. This is where you say, 'I bet you won't,' Carmen."

She laughed. "Thanks for saying it for me. And am I allowed to also say that I'm really happy about this, Katie? You're such a bright girl, and you know it. Cormack and I will do whatever we can to help."

At that moment she would have promised her sister the moon, she was so relieved. Since she didn't actually own the moon, she began to plan ways to budget for some more modest forms of assistance instead, wishing the way she'd wished for years that she could do a heck of a lot more.

Jack was up on his roof, clearing out the gutters, when Terri showed up early to pick up Ryan on a Wednesday afternoon. She took in his dirt- and paint-stained work attire, and the sandpaper and scrapers still sitting on the front porch after the preparation he'd being doing on the window frames earlier. "Does this mean you're still not back at work, after all this time?" she yelled up at him.

"Next week," he told her, backing carefully onto the ladder and starting the downward climb. He'd used up all his accumulated vacation days, and knew they'd been well spent.

"Does your boss know you've been using the time this way?"

"How was I supposed to use it?"

"Recuperating, surely."

"This is recuperating." He felt so much better than he had a few weeks ago, no more nightmares about the dead woman or her gun, no jaw aching from clenching it without knowing. He'd talked several times to his partner, Russ, on the phone, and last week they'd gone out for a drink. Somehow an energetic discussion about sports and no personal conversation at all had led each of them to the conclusion that the other one was doing okay.

"I don't see how," Terri said.

"So I guess it's lucky you're not a police staff psychologist." He reached the bottom of the ladder and she stepped quickly back, as if the blotches of dried paint on his jeans might make a flying leap onto her burgundy suit. Apparently, she didn't intend making a retort to his last comment, so he added, "You're early, Terri."

"Forty minutes. I was in the area."

No. She was checking him out. Did Jack let their son

plug himself into electronic games all afternoon? Did he pay the kid any attention? How many freshly emptied soda cans were lying in the new kitchen sink?

Jack knew this the way he knew his own name, but swallowed the challenge that almost escaped his lips, and told her, "Ryan's still eating his after-school snack. Come in. He's been so hungry this week. I swear he was a half inch taller this morning than when he went to bed last night."

Terri's habitual and very obvious prickle of distrust softened a little. "Oh, tell me about it! We saw a great pony for him on the weekend but I had to say to the seller it would probably be too small for him in less than a year. We—"

She stopped suddenly as she realized what she'd said. Her face flamed and she took a breath ready to gabble something out, but Jack got in first.

"You looked at ponies."

She said quickly, "Nothing's decided yet."

"Something's decided," he said sharply. "Ryan's going to change his name and get his own horse for a reward."

"No, Jack, no!" She looked genuinely stricken. He still knew her pretty well, and he could tell the difference between when she was playing games and when she really felt something. This time her protest and her concern was real. "I meant, that's *not* decided, yet. He seriously hasn't made up his mind, and we don't want to force the issue."

"So dangling actual ponies in front of him, in the flesh, complete with shaggy manes and leathery pony

smells and names like Shadow or Comanche or Flint…
That isn't forcing the issue?"

She bit her lip, her face still flaming with guilt and
regret. "All right. I guess it could look that way, but that
wasn't the intention, Jack, honestly. Jay's been looking
on the Internet. He thought we should go see some. To
get an idea. So that if Ryan does decide to go in that direction, we've already done the research. Ryan is taking
this very seriously. He cares about you so much. And
no matter what doubts I might have about your priorities and goals in certain areas, I know how hard
you're trying and how much you want to be the right
kind of father to him. I didn't mention the pony thing
to scare you. I didn't intend to mention it at all."

"But it slipped out."

"Yes, it did." Her blue gaze swept over him. He'd
thought there could be nothing worse in their relationship than the manipulation and the games and the hostility, but now he discovered he'd been wrong. What he
saw in her eyes now was worse.

Pity.

She honestly thought that he was a failure. She
honestly wanted to *protect* him from feeling deeply in-
adequate in the face of Jay Kruger's wealth and class
and background and success.

And the really sickening part about it was that when
she looked at him that way, when she spoke to him with
that damned aura of *kindness* in her face and tone, he
started to buy into the same attitude.

Maybe she was right.

Maybe his simple values didn't even begin to stack up against what Jay had and what he could offer their son.

Maybe winning really was everything, nice guys always did finish last, and what every woman really did want was a man with a private jet and a deck of platinum credit cards. Honest hands and a true heart just weren't enough.

"Get him the pony," he told Terri, as she followed him into the house, where Ryan should just be finishing up an apple and a peanut butter sandwich. "That's what he wants. Ryan Kruger sounds just as good as Ryan Davey. I'm not going to stand in his way."

"Can I show you something, Carmen?" Cormack appeared halfway down the stairs.

It was four in the afternoon. They'd finished a big bathroom renovation just before three, and at that hour, after beginning work at seven this morning, it hadn't been worth starting on their next scheduled project, which was a forty-five-minute drive away. Instead, they'd come home early, and Cormack had been doing some business admin in the small back bedroom he and Carmen used as an office. Now, he looked tense and uneasy.

"Sure," Carmen answered casually, as if she hadn't noticed the uneasiness. She would wait until she understood the problem before getting anxious or letting it show. Surely the business wasn't in trouble? She followed him up to the office.

But he paused on the landing before he got there. "How're things going with you and Jack, by the way?"

It wasn't the kind of question Cormack usually asked about her personal life, the way she wouldn't have asked a similar question to him. They were close, but not heart-to-heart close. More like quietly-watch-out-for-each-other close.

Mel was the sibling she usually confided in, and yet she hadn't told Mel much about Jack yet, either. Just that she was seeing a guy who'd started out as a client a couple of months ago. But they'd finished the final touches on Jack's kitchen and downstairs bathroom now, so the client thing wasn't an issue anymore. In fact, it really hadn't been an issue from the beginning.

To herself, she kept her instinctive, gut-level sense of how important this could be, her sense that Jack felt the same way, and her sense of fragility and fear, too. With Terri and Jay and Ryan in the picture, as well as her own complicated family situation, she didn't dare to breathe easy too soon, nor did she feel like shouting anything from the rooftops. When two stranded swimmers locked their arms around each other for support, they could drag each other down instead of floating.

She stopped and took a good look at Cormack before she answered his question. He had a pen sticking between two fingers and he was flipping it, making it twirl back and forth so fast it turned into a blur.

There was something forbidding about the way he stood and the way he looked, with his strong build and dark hair. Something hard edged. She thought that someday the right woman would manage to bring out his innate generosity and warmth and staying power—*tame* him, if you wanted to put it that way—but this day was still a long way off. For the past ten years or more, the longest he'd dated any one woman was less than three months. He'd broken more Jersey Girl hearts than Carmen could count.

What kind of an answer did he want to his out-of-character question, she wondered. The honest kind, or the guy kind—one throwaway syllable.

She opted for the latter. "Fine." But spoiled the effect when she added, "Why?"

No answer.

They reached the office and he picked up a letter from the bank. "This came today. Jack's final payment check for the renovation bounced."

*"Bounced?"*

"That's what I said."

"The final payment was for, what, a third of the total?" They almost always invoiced for a job in thirds.

"Two-thirds." Before she could query his correction, he added, "When the second payment was due, Jack asked me if he could lump it in with the final one. You were already going out with him then, he seemed like a trustworthy guy and he had some story about the medical bills from the shooting. Insurance claims getting delayed or something."

"Two-thirds," she echoed, doing the math in her head and registering those words, *some story*. Clearly, Cormack didn't believe the story anymore. Did she?

"Yeah," he said. "Two-thirds, on a complete kitchen and a substantial-sized half bath. It's a fair bit of money, Carmen."

Money that they couldn't afford to shrug over or wait for, especially when Carmen knew she'd probably lie awake for hours tonight, with her head going round and round as she thought about how best to get Kate through eight years of expensive college degrees.

"So what's going on?" Cormack looked at her.

"You're asking me as if I'd know." She added quickly, "Okay, okay, I'm seeing him. It's a reasonable question. But he hasn't said anything."

"So this is the first you've heard of him having money problems?"

"He…he doesn't have money problems. I'm sure he doesn't."

Cormack looked at her with a wooden expression, and Carmen knew what he wanted her to say.

So she said it. "I'll go over there right now and see if I can find out what's happened."

"Yeah, would you?"

"It's what you hoped I'd say, isn't it?"

"But I won't push you if it's awkward."

"Having our own payment checks to our suppliers bouncing because we don't have money in the bank is going to be more awkward."

Cormack watched her for a moment in silence, and Carmen hoped he couldn't see how much she was already dreading what she had to do.

* * *

Pulling into his driveway, she found Terri's car parked there. Her heart lurched and sank. Great. Just great: several minutes of being polite to Jack's ex before she could get down to a piece of business she didn't want to conduct in the first place.

But why was Terri looking up at the house, with her car keys in one hand and the other hand shading her eyes?

Carmen soon saw the reason.

Jack was on the roof.

She climbed out of the car. He'd seen her, she thought, but he didn't acknowledge her presence.

"You couldn't wait until we left before you went back up there?" Terri called to him. Ryan stood beside her with his backpack dangling in his hand. He'd been staying here for his usual weeknights with his dad, and Terri had come to take him home.

"I want to get this done before the light starts to go," Jack yelled in reply. "It's nothing personal, Terri." He caught Carmen's eye and waved at her. She flicked her fingers back to him, feeling her stomach churn.

Ryan saw her and said, "Hi, Carmen."

She wanted to ruffle his head or something. He reminded her of her brother Joe, who was seven years younger than she was. When Joe was Ryan's age, she'd already been a surrogate mother to him for two years. But with Terri around, she always felt less able to show her growing affection for Jack's son, so all she said was, "Hi, big guy."

"Dad's on the roof."

"Yeah, I see him up there. What's he doing?"

"Clearing out the gutters. And doing tricks."

"Tricks?"

Ryan called up to Jack. "Dad, do the tightrope walk again!"

"Ryan, honey, no," Terri said. "No more stupid stunts. We have things we need to get done. We have to leave."

"Okay," Ryan answered, resigned but grumbling. He was about to turn toward the car, but then his face broke into a broad grin. "Look, Carmen, he's doing it! Look how fast he is!"

Jack walked the ridgeline of the sloping roof, his arms held out sideways for balance, his pose casual and his steps quick and confident. For one moment, he teetered, but then regained his balance, turned back the way he'd come and took a bow. "Ta-da!"

He grinned down at Ryan, who went, "Yay, Dad!" and laughed and clapped before Terri hustled him into the car. She had her lips pressed tightly together, as if she'd seen the tightrope routine many times before and wasn't impressed.

For Carmen, it was flashback time.

Rainy night—a summer storm. Nine-year-old Joe had just started Little League that year, and was due to be picked up from practice. But as usual Dad had been drinking. Carmen and Cormack both knew it. Cormack had just gotten his learners' permit a week before, and he couldn't drive in weather like this. He could barely reverse safely down the drive.

"I'll go get him on my bicycle," Carmen said. "I

tried a couple of the Little League parents, but no one was picking up." This was before most people had cell phones.

"You'll have to sneak out," Cormack warned her. "If Dad knows Joe needs picking up, he'll want to go."

Too late.

Dad had one of his erratic spurts of responsibility and remembered that he'd seen Joe taking his Little League gear to school with him that morning, and that practice finished at five. He announced, with the car keys in his hand, that he was leaving now to pick him up.

"No, Dad," Cormack tried to say. "Carmen's going for him on her bicycle."

Dad wouldn't listen. Didn't they see that rain? Cormack held up the empty beer and whisky bottles, but Dad insisted he was fine. He was never anything but fine, according to him, while they could see him unraveling day by day.

And then Cormack tried to make him prove that he wasn't too drunk to drive by insisting that he walk a straight line, following the grouting in the tiles on the kitchen floor. Dad wove his way along it with his arms held out like wobbly wings, crowing, "Straight as a die, boy, straight as a die," while Carmen, with one of those left-field thoughts—why did they happen and why did she remember this detail?—stood there wondering, what's a die? Is it die? Or dye? What is it, and why is it so straight?

Dad's line wasn't remotely straight, it weaved and stopped and weaved again, but he had the car keys and

Cormack wasn't strong enough to snatch them by brute force—Carmen could see how bad he felt that his attempt at reasoning with their father had failed—so they waited twenty-five minutes with hearts in their mouths while the rain poured down outside, for Dad to bring little Joey safely home.

Somehow he managed it.

He was still crowing to them two hours later, even drunker by this time, about walking a straight line.

And there was Jack on the ridge of the roof, thirty feet from the ground, grinning down at her with his hands on his hips, while she watched him with the letter from the bank about his bounced check burning a hole in her pocket. He saw Terri's car turn out of the driveway, and the grin drained from his face like water down a pipe.

"I'll be down in a minute," he said.

He looked tense, suddenly, his whole body tight and crackling and just not happy. That tightrope thing had only been a performance. Maybe he knew why she was here. The bank had probably sent him a letter about the check, also. Maybe the whole stunt had been nothing more than a piece of bravado for Carmen's benefit before he faced the music.

Terri certainly hadn't been impressed about it.

*And Terri is right about Jack sometimes,* came the traitorous thought. Carmen felt like a stranded swimmer again, tied to him with her whole heart and her whole body. Tied to him and drowning as she tried to save them both.

"What's up?" he said, when he reached the ground. "Do I look as if something's up?"

"Yes," he said bluntly. "You do. And you don't usually play those *I'm not upset* games, so spill." He softened the words by reaching out to touch her, but she leaned away from the caress and he dropped his hand. They stood there, the awareness and need to touch crackling between them like a jet of lightning. Magnetic lightning. It burned and wouldn't let go.

He looked tired. Defeated, almost. The laugh lines around his mouth had deepened into tight brackets and his eyes were narrowed with tension. He'd been seriously, expertly faking that "stunt" up on the roof, which didn't stop the powerful memory of Carmen's drunken father in the kitchen, jeering at Cormack in his slurred voice for making him walk the line.

She wanted to tell Jack, never mind what's getting to me, what's gotten to you? But she was here on a mission—a business errand, an emotional confrontation—and she couldn't get the echo of her dad and that line of tile grouting out of her head. "Your check for the kitchen and bathroom work bounced," she said.

Either Jack hadn't looked at his own mail yet, or he was giving another convincing performance. "No! That can't be right."

"I brought the letter from the bank."

"I'm not saying you've got it wrong, Carmen. But the bank has. I'm sure. There should have been enough in the account. I made sure of that." He looked at her more closely, saw how angry and tight she was. "We'll clear this up," he promised. He reached for her again, pressed her cold hand between his and chafed at it as if trying to warm it up.

"Good." Their eyes met and held a kiss that didn't happen. Couldn't happen. She was crazy to want it.

"Your reaction seems a little out of proportion for what was an honest mistake," he said. He took another look at her face. "Except that you don't think this was an honest mistake, do you?"

"I— You've been doing all that trading on the Internet. You told me a couple of weeks ago that you'd lost five hundred dollars on it. Dad used to bet on the races when he was drunk. Crazy amounts that were going to pay off big and somehow make everything right, make Mom's death not matter anymore."

"So now you think I have a gambling problem, too? You and Terri, both. The amount of trust and faith you don't have in me—" He shook his head in disgust.

"I'm not like Terri."

"No?"

"I wish I was. She let you go. I don't think I can."

"Oh, hell, Carmen…" he whispered.

Without her knowing how it had happened, he was kissing her, deep and hungry and hot, and she parted her lips to let him in, tasting the familiar freshness of his mouth, feeling his body hard against her. She tried to gather enough willpower to push him away, because she knew there was more to say—more to yell, more to forgive—but she couldn't do it. The feeling of belonging in his arms was so strong, even when it had no power to make her happy.

"How do we get to a better place, Jack?" she murmured, in the brief space he left for her to breathe. She didn't actually want to breathe or need to breathe right now. She needed to understand the things that trapped them both.

"We talk," he said, then he kissed her again and they couldn't talk.

They didn't want to. They wanted to pull each other's clothes off and stumble to his bed. The couch. The carpet. Anywhere.

From some unknown well of strength inside her, Carmen found what she needed to free herself from the drugging heat and pressure of his body.

"Kate wants to go back to college," she said. "We're not exactly operating on a gushing cash flow, Jack. I had to tell Cormack I was sure this was just some tiny mistake. He's wondering if you're trading on the fact that you and I—"

"The check should have cleared," he cut in, angry and stubborn. His eyes burned and glittered, and she felt so lost—set adrift by the fact that she couldn't trust him, whether the distrust was her problem or his. "I hate that you instantly conclude I have major financial problems because of one glitch."

"And I hate what you were doing on the roof," she blurted out.

He turned away from her and muttered under his breath. "I don't need this today."

"And you think I do? You think this was my idea of a

fun afternoon, to come here and tell the new man in my life, hey, what happened to payment for honest work?"

"There was enough in the account."

"I hate talking this way," she said hotly. "Accusations about money."

And you. So like my dad. Thinking that walking one straight line, on a roof or a kitchen floor, makes you a man.

How did that Johnny Cash song go?

"You think I'm enjoying it?" Jack drawled.

"It wouldn't be happening at all, if—" She stopped. If he took more care. If he listened to her fear.

"If what?" He looked ominous, now, not threatening her but threatening himself, almost, as if he might just crack completely and go punching walls, breaking his hand, get himself arrested by one of his fellow cops for some piece of out-of-control behavior.

It scared her that she didn't know him well enough to trust how far he would or wouldn't go. Where was his breaking point? Why did he seem so close to reaching it?

*I can't go there again.*

She knew it, suddenly, the way she knew Cormack's silences and Kate's teenage tantrums.

She could not tie her heart and her life and her well-being to a man who reminded her so much of her dad, no matter how strong the pull toward him. She could not live through the fear or the anger or the picking up pieces of another person's emotional mess. She was still picking up pieces—Kate's pieces—and she just did not have the strength or the courage to sign up for more of the same, when it might never end.

"It doesn't matter," she told him.

"What doesn't matter?"

"How the mistake happened with the check, or why you were teetering along that roof, showing off to your son when, from the look on your face the second he and Terri left, it was the last thing in the world you felt like doing. Jack, I can't do this. I can't keep seeing you. I want to. So much. But I can't. It'll hurt and scar both of us too much."

He swallowed and nodded. Didn't speak.

"I don't expect you to understand. I'm just…tired, or something."

"Kate?"

"Kate. Not just Kate."

"Ryan."

"Ryan. Terri. Memories of my dad. All along we've both known—" she took a breath "—how much more complicated it is to hold on to a connection when there are so many other people involved. And I can't do it. I think I told you I could. Mothers-in-law from hell and pet rats. But I was wrong. I guess I'm not strong enough. Say something, Jack."

"What is there to say? You want me to argue?"

And a part of her did.

A huge part of her wanted him to sweep her off her feet the way he had a minute ago when he'd kissed her, only this time with watertight, ironclad reasons for the bounced check, the stunt on the roof—all the reasons why he was nothing like her dad, why everything in their lives was simple and easy and already solved.

Sweep her off her feet and into his arms where she could stay forever, and where she would never know the burdens of anger and fear and lack of trust again.

But she knew it wasn't going to happen.

He knew it, too.

From his face, he knew it better than she did. He didn't even begin to try, didn't touch her or kiss her or inflame her body with all those powerful reminders of the strength of their connection that he could have used.

"No," she said. "I don't want you to argue."

"Didn't think so."

"I'd better go."

"I'll call Cormack when I find out what happened with that check."

"Thanks."

On legs that felt half-numb, she walked back to the car, opened the door, strapped herself in, started the engine. Then she looked along the driveway, expecting to find him still watching her. But he was nowhere in sight. He'd gone back into the house, as if the aching pull still dragging between them was only in her mind.

## Chapter Ten

Jack felt like an old man as he went into the house. His body ached with the effort of keeping his emotions in check. Police counselor's advice or no police counselor's advice, however, he wasn't going to let the floodgates open today.

As usual, he needed action.

First task, find out why the hell his check for the renovation hadn't cleared.

Second task, cancel his Internet share trading account, before his losing battle to match up to what Ryan was being taught to value in a man got him into serious financial trouble.

*Kid, I love you more than anything else in the world, but I can't be someone I'm not. I don't want to be someone I'm not. My pride in who I am has been knocked around a heck of a lot lately, by your mother and your stepdad, but if I'm going back to square one, then it's my own square one, not anybody else's.*

The solution to problem number one turned out to be, of all things, Barbie.

Yup, the trademarked blonde with the cute outfits that little girls loved. That Barbie.

More than two months ago, Jack had sent a check for a pair of new Barbie dolls to his sister Laura in Florida for her twin daughters' shared birthday but she'd forgotten to bank it until the week before last and he hadn't realized. The price of two extravagantly dressed collector's edition dolls had been just enough to put his checking account temporarily in the red once the payment to C & C Renovations came into the equation.

The solution to problem number two was even easier.

He canceled the share account and felt a weight of expectation lift from his shoulders. He was never going to get rich on the stock market. In fact, he was never going to get rich, period. He was simply going to do the best he could as a New Jersey cop, give things to Ryan that he valued far more than money—time, laughter, ideas—and make his house into his own kind of palace with the labor of his own two hands. He was stubbornly going to believe that the world was a tiny bit of a better place because he was in it, and to hell with prestige schools and platinum credit cards and bribing kids with ponies.

Only two things hurt.

Ryan.

Carmen.

Not necessarily in that order.

"Had a call from Jack just now," Cormack said casually to Carmen.

It was Friday, two days since he'd told her about the bounced check, two days since she'd told Jack she couldn't see him anymore. She hadn't told Cormack about Jack, but he'd probably guessed. Kate might have guessed, also. Puffy eyes, no appetite, too much time spent in the bathroom rinsing a tear-stained face. Carmen had barely eaten and her stomach felt queasy.

"Oh, yes? What did he say?" she asked.

They were sitting in the spring sunshine on a bench in the garden belonging to their current kitchen client, eating their lunch. Carmen had a tuna salad wrap. *Why,* said her stomach. *Why* did you think a tuna salad wrap would work? It's not going to! Get it out of my sight now!

Cormack had a burger and fries. She put the quarter-eaten wrap back in its paper bag and stole one of the fries, and the salt hit her tongue like a knight in shining armor galloping to rescue a princess. It was the first thing that had tasted good in days.

"He's put the money for the renovation straight into our business account via electronic transfer. I checked over the phone and it's there."

"What was the problem before? Did he say?"

"Something about a birthday check to his sister that he'd forgotten, or she'd forgotten, I can't remember. The money's in, that's all I care about."

"Sometimes, Cormack, you bug the hell out of me, you know that!" She stole another fry.

"Yeah, but when I hug you and get all sympathetic," he said gruffly, "you just start to cry." So he had noticed.... "And you've done enough of that the past couple of days."

He proved his point by putting an arm around her shoulders and roughing up her hair in a gesture of brotherly love, which did indeed make her cry. "Anyhow, it wasn't just the money, was it?" he added.

"No."

"Do I have to kill him for you?"

"Yeah, Corm, thanks, that'd be peachy. Going to visit you in jail because you're serving life for murder, while I'm running the business on my own and putting Kate through med school." The salt from the third stolen fry hit her tongue.

"Just thought I should make the offer."

She swallowed. "You're good to me."

"So what was it that messed everything up?" he asked tentatively. "You two looked good together, I thought."

"Boy, you are in touch with your feminine side today!"

"Yeah, but it won't last, so if you want to talk, take the window while you can."

"He reminded me of Dad," she said simply.

Silence, then a big whoosh of breath. "That is the last thing I expected you to say."

"Or I reminded me of myself, dreading Dad, not trusting him, being so angry, almost hating him. Dad, I mean."

"Hating him for not being stronger."

"Yes."

"Jack seems incredibly strong to me."

"Strong and reckless."

"No."

"You haven't seen it, Cormack. You weren't there when he—"

"Okay, the window of femininity is closing fast. I think you're making too big of a deal about this. Jack is not like Dad. I'm not going to analyze it or pick apart every single little thing he's done and every particle of emotion in how you've reacted. I was there, remember? When Dad was self-destructing? He gave up. He didn't even try."

"Yes, and—"

"What did Jack do when he got shot? He began renovating his house with his own hands. What did he do when he got divorced? He busted his guts to get more time with his son. How in the heck does any of that remind you of Dad?"

Carmen shrugged. Her stomach felt fragile again. "So maybe it's me," she said. "Maybe I'm never going to feel as safe with a man as I need to feel. Maybe I'm always going to get scared and angry because it feels as if I'm standing on the shakiest of ground, all on my own. The end result is the same. It doesn't work. It can't work."

"I like Jack," Cormack said stubbornly, as if this was all that mattered. "He's a good guy."

His feminine-side window had definitely closed.

"Well, good for you," Carmen told him. "I'm going to go measure some walls."

\* \* \*

The queasy feeling refused to go away.

It was bad in the mornings after she'd lain awake for hours in the night, aching for Jack. It was worse when the phone rang and she thought with a lurching heart that it might be him. It was worst of all when she was tired after a hard day's work and just wanted to sleep for a hundred years.

Despite being at least another eight and a half years away from being able to call herself a doctor, Kate was the one who diagnosed the problem.

"Did I hear you throwing up in the bathroom this morning..."

"I'm sorry, I couldn't manage to shut the—"

"*...again?*"

"I guess it's three times, now," Carmen conceded. *See what you've done to me, Jack Davey?*

"So are you pregnant?" Kate fixed her with a stare of beady-eyed curiosity. "Have you done a test?"

*"Pregnant?"*

The dropped jaw probably looked comical from Kate's angle. With exaggerated patience, she told her big sister, "Yeah, Carmie, little-known side effect of having sex. We learned about it in biology, at school. You should have paid more attention. I can get hold of some crib notes, if you want."

"But we used contra—" She stopped.

Kate was blocking her ears with her hands. "Too much detail. Too, too much." She took her hands away and said, "I mean, maybe you're not, but it's a possibility you could consider exploring, don't you think?" She grinned suddenly. "I will be soooo evilly pleased if we have a major role reversal, here, and it's the wise, nagging Carmen in this situation instead of the irresponsible teen sister."

Carmen closed her eyes. "Don't be a brat. Not now. Please?" Tears squeezed onto her cheeks.

She felt Kate's arms fold around her back, and heard her stricken tone. "Carmie, what's wrong? Oh, shoot, I wouldn't have teased you about it like that if I'd thought it was such bad news. I know I'm a brat. I am a brat. A total brat. I'm sorry!"

"I told him I couldn't see him anymore."

"No!"

Carmen nodded. Yes.

"But you really care about him. I can see you do, or you wouldn't be hurting like this."

"That doesn't mean he's good for me."

"You've looked so happy when you've been with him. All bright-eyed and your earrings jiggling every time you move your head."

*"What?"*

"Your earrings. When you're happy—or busy— you move your head faster and they jiggle. I've seen him watching them. Jack. He thinks they're hot. He thinks *you're* hot, and you are, and he cares about you. A lot."

"Even if that's true—"

"Of course it's true! I don't understand why you're doing this to yourself."

Most of the time Carmen didn't understand it, either. Fear was like that. You just ran from the source of the terror. You couldn't think. You couldn't stop. Sometimes you couldn't even breathe.

Kate didn't let go of the hug. She rubbed Carmen's back, making helpless, stricken little sounds. It was the first time in their lives, Carmen realized, that their roles had been reversed—that Carmen had cried and Kate had comforted, that Kate had stood helplessly by while Carmen messed everything up.

"The idea of a baby scares me so much," she whispered to her baby sister.

"But you're so great with kids. You'll make a fabulous mom. You've had so much practice."

"Yeah, I have. Exactly. Half a lifetime of it. And you think I'm ready for another eighteen or twenty years, without time to pause for breath?"

"Oh, jeesh…!" Kate breathed, her body stiffening as she understood what Carmen was saying.

She cut in quickly, "Katie, I'm not saying I've hated it or resented it—resented *you,* or Mel or Joe. I haven't. But it's been so hard, sometimes. I've hated Dad, I've been so angry with him."

"*Hated* him?"

Kate had been too young. Her memories were the good ones, and Carmen had never shared her own blunt, uncompromising knowledge that Dad had killed himself on that wet road because he hadn't had the strength or the courage or the love to keep himself safe for their sakes.

Maybe it was time for Kate to know.

"For abandoning us. He didn't take care of himself. That whole year between when Mom died and when he went off the bridge, he was an accident waiting to happen. And it did happen. And it wouldn't have, if he'd put his priority on taking care of his five mother-less kids, instead of on drowning his grief in drink." She was sobbing now. "He was an adult. A man. And he couldn't step up to the plate. And I have *glued* myself to that plate, and so has Cormack, because we refused to do what Dad did. We just refused."

"And I've spat in your face about a thousand times. I haven't helped. I've been horrible."

"You're a teenager, Katie, it's your job."

"Not anymore, Carmie. You don't know how I used to play the orphan card at school." She shook her head, disgusted at herself. "I never thought, not really, never sat down and put myself in your shoes, or Cormack's, and thought that you were orphans, too, and you had it so much harder."

"In some ways. But not all. I had two parents for fourteen years of my childhood. You had them for just four. You had it hard, too, Katie, so don't start beating yourself up just because I'm talking to you like this."

"Let me beat myself up, if you're not going to do it for me."

"Don't. I'd rather have your energy for better things."

"Yeah?"

"Yes! If I'm pregnant now, I'll love the baby with my whole soul, I'll glue myself to that plate again. I'll love a baby with everything I've got. But I'm scared. About the weight of it. Because I know how the weight feels, when you're almost on your own."

"I'll help, Carmie. I'll walk the floor and change diapers and push the stroller for miles while you take naps."

Carmen laughed. "I haven't taken a test yet!"

"So I'll jump in the car right now and go to the drug-store to pick one up."

She did.

She even paid for it, because Carmen forgot to give her the money.

And the result was positive.

The first thing that Carmen knew for certain after this, amongst the whirling mess of her thoughts and feelings, was that she had to call Jack and give him the news.

"I want to get a job," Ryan said.

He and Jack sat at a restaurant booth on Friday night, eating chicken pot pies with no side orders so they could save room for all-you-can-eat dessert. The job announcement came from left field, as so many of Ryan's opening conversational gambits seemed to do. Jack had learned a degree of wariness in his initial response.

"Oh, yeah?" he said.

"Am I allowed to?"

"Depends on the job."

"Just something that earns money."

"Well, that sure narrows it down."

"Like, that a kid can do. Like feeding people's pets when they're away or cutting grass or something."

"Those you could probably handle." He wanted to ask if Jay had something to do with this new ambition.

What did Ryan have to "earn" now?

But he made himself stay silent until he'd worked out how to get the information without turning it into a challenge to Ryan's loyalties. He was still struggling for the right angle when Ryan spoke again.

"Because I want to pay for a pony myself."

"Pay for a pony?"

"I told Jay already. He says he's okay with it. I'm keeping Davey."

"You're keeping Davey."

Ah, hell, Jack, stop sounding like a parrot!

"Jay said, 'Well, son, that's your choice and it's a fine name.' And he said he and Mom would revisit the pony issue, and I said, which pony, the one we saw on the weekend, because I wanted to come, too, when they revisited it, and he said he didn't mean revisit that way, he meant maybe I could have a pony after all, even staying Ryan Davey, but I said no."

"How come you said no?"

Ryan shrugged and turned his mouth upside down. "It kind of felt like they'd tricked me, Mom and Jay, even if it turned out to be a nice trick. They said I could only have a pony if I changed my name, so why did they say I could still have one when I decided not to change my name?"

Why, indeed?

Jack recognized Terri's hand in the whole thing. She changed her own rules all the time, the way she changed outfits and shoes. Mix 'n' match, depending on her whims and moods. She'd probably intended for Ryan to get his pony all along, and hadn't considered that he might call her bluff by resisting the bribe.

"I'm proud of you," he blurted out to his son, knowing he sounded a little too emotional. Kids didn't *get* that stuff. They had no idea how important they were in a parent's eyes. How could they?

"Ahh, Dad, I knew you'd say that."

"You did?"

He shrugged again. "I know you're proud of me."

"Well, good. A kid should know that. You must be disappointed about the pony, though. A little?"

Third shrug. "That's why I'm going to get a job."

Subject closed, apparently.

Jack kept his expression as neutral as he could. He still felt too emotional. There'd been a feeling like a stone in his gut since Wednesday, when he and Carmen had called it quits, and even though his pride and love for Ryan was a heck of a lot more comfortable than the stone, the feelings still shook him up.

*I've done something right.*

*I must have done something right with my son, because Ryan has made exactly the decision I wanted him to make, all on his own.*

He remembered that his first instinct when he'd been angry about the pony weeks ago had been to call Carmen, and so help him he wanted to do the same today. It hurt that he couldn't do it—hurt in some deep, sickening way that he didn't have words to describe.

He choked his way through the potpie and all-you-can-eat dessert, and managed not to have Ryan see how churned up he was inside.

There was a message from Carmen on his answering machine when the two of them got home. As soon as Ryan's head hit the pillow, Jack called her back.

Carmen couldn't tell Jack the news about the baby over the phone. She had thought she would be able to, that the physical distance of a phone call might provide a kind of protection for both of them, but when it came to the crunch…

Nope. Wasn't going to happen. They were both too awkward and unhappy, and when she couldn't see him or touch him or measure exactly what he was feeling…

No.

"Is everything okay, Jack?" she asked instead.

"Ryan's just gone to bed. I'm not sure if he's asleep yet."

"Meaning you have something to tell me about him, and you don't want to risk him hearing?"

"Something like that. About the pony."

"I want to see you, Jack," she blurted out. "I need to. I— Yeah. There's…oh, Lord…unfinished business." She almost had to laugh at putting it this way.

"Not the kind I can transfer electronically into your bank account, I'm guessing."

"No. But thanks for putting in the payment so promptly. Cormack was pleased."

"No problem, Carmen. Is it the kind of unfinished business we can deal with over coffee or dinner?"

"We can start."

*"Start?"*

"Let's try dinner," she said quickly.

"When?"

"Sunday? After you take Ryan home?"

"The unfinished business must be pretty important."

She didn't reply. Was still trying to frame some words—any words—when he spoke again.

"Okay, make it Sunday," he said. "I won't push you on it now. I'll pick you up. Seven?"

"Seven is good."

"I'll tell you about the pony then."

*And I'll tell you about the baby…*

## Chapter Eleven

"Hey, big fella!" Ryan's stepfather gave his shoulder a squeeze.

"Hi, Jay. Bye, Dad."

Ryan sensed dinner about to be served, Jack guessed.

The kid catapulted past Jay at the open doorway and into the big front hallway of the magnificent Kruger home. He dumped his backpack at the foot of the sweeping curved staircase and disappeared in the direction of the huge, restaurant-quality kitchen to find out what smelled so good. Apparently Terri still cooked most Sunday nights, although she had her housekeeper prepare it or else they dined out for the rest of the week.

To Jack, it seemed like another world.

On the one hand, he liked the fact that Ryan seemed

to take these transitions between the very different Kruger and Davey lifestyles in stride. On the other, the hi-Jay-bye-Dad routine suggested that Ryan's two homes, two lives and two dads were almost interchangeable, which wasn't such a pleasing thought.

"Did he have a good weekend?" Jay asked Jack. He was a neatly built, conservatively dressed man of almost forty, his hair already turned gray. Jack towered over him by several inches, but Jay's sense of entitlement and power spoke in a hundred subtle ways. A stranger would probably have no trouble picking the corporate mogul from the cop.

"Yep," Jack said, forcing down his habitual discomfort. "We went to a baseball game, threw a few balls around the yard ourselves. I've given him a bed of dirt as his own in the garden, and we're planting some vegetables."

"Good. That sounds great." Jay gave a short, approving nod. "Kids can learn a lot that way."

"That, too," Jack agreed, because he and Ryan were doing the vegetable garden for fun more than education.

He made a move to leave. Neither Terri nor Jay ever invited him inside, which was fine because he didn't usually invite Terri into his place, either. They handled the situation better than those divorced parents whose hostility level was so high they had to swap the kids around in a parking lot outside a fast-food restaurant, but all the same, he and Jay weren't exactly friends.

So it was a surprise when Jay said, "Hang on, there, Jack, let's talk for a moment."

"Sure." He paused and waited.

"Want to come in for a drink?"

"I would, but I have to be somewhere pretty soon."

At Carmen's, in twenty minutes, to pick her up for the dinner date that was making the jitters breed like rabbits in his stomach. He had no idea what she wanted to say, except that, after the way they'd parted on Wednesday, she wouldn't be saying it if it wasn't important.

"Okay, then I'll make it quick," Jay promised.

"Go ahead," he invited, instinctively wary as to what "it" might be.

"You're a good father, Jack."

"Wh—"

Jay let out a laugh when he saw Jack's expression. "Don't look as if you're waiting for the other shoe to drop."

"But it's going to, isn't it?"

"Not sure how you'll react, actually." He grinned. "Me, I'm over the moon."

Was this still about the pony? Wasn't that off the agenda for the time being?

"Terri wanted me to tell you," Jay went on. "She's pregnant. We wanted to play it safe and get some testing done before we told anybody, but we've gotten the results back now and everything's normal. It's a boy, due at the end of November."

"Congratulations. That's great."

"And when I heard the news I realized how much pressure I'd been putting on my relationship with Ryan over the past couple of years."

Ah.

"But soon you'll have a son of your own to carry on the Kruger name and traditions, so you won't need my son for the role," Jack guessed aloud. "Is that what you're saying?"

"I won't need to *pressure* him into the role," Jay corrected. "Which I'd been doing without fully realizing it, and if you resented it…" he stuck out his hand abruptly, for Jack to shake. He did so, and they pumped heartily up and down like the presidents of two hostile nations at a peace conference, mugging for the cameras "…well, you had a good case, and I owe you an apology." Jay dropped his hand at last. "Ryan is a fine boy, and I care about him."

"Not quite the way I do," Jack growled.

Jay gave another nod. "He's right to keep his loyalty with you, his father, and I admire him for doing so. He won't lose out here once the new baby is born. You have the Kruger word on that. As I said, you're a good father. I only hope I'm one, too."

It sounded a little rehearsed, a little forced, a little pompous, but Jack took it in the spirit it was meant, and mangled his way through some gruff thanks and more congratulations. "Have you told Ryan?" he asked.

"Not yet. How do you think he'll take it?"

"A little wary at first, I guess, but he'll love the baby to pieces once he's born." He had to fight a grin, thinking about it. Judging by the way Ryan treated Tux, he would make a great big brother.

"That's what Terri says." Jay was grinning now, too.

"Yes, there are still one or two things she and I agree

on," Jack drawled. He looked at his watch, and Jay registered the action.

"You need to get going," he said. "I won't keep you."

"Give my congrats to Terri."

"She'll be pleased."

She'd been hiding, Jack realized.

Usually, she was the one to come to the door when he brought Ryan home. She hadn't known how he'd react to the baby news, so she'd deputized Jay to deliver it. She must have known or suspected her pregnancy that day more than two months ago when she'd told Jack he could have Ryan five nights out of fourteen—the day he'd met Carmen—so there had been more than one piece of hidden motivation going on behind her actions lately.

She needn't have worried about the ramifications of the coming baby. On the whole, Jack believed Jay's assurances that this would take some pressure from Ryan's shoulders. Maybe, with a new baby in the house, Terri would even agree to a more equal division of Ryan's time.

He drove to Carmen's with new determination surging through him. Whatever her reason for wanting to see him tonight, he was going to turn it to what he wanted, and what he knew they could have.

Jack had never seen her this dressed up, Carmen realized.

When she opened the door to him in her swishy, figure-hugging red dress, she saw the flash in his eyes. Then he whistled. Her skin began to tingle and the constant, relentless, instinctive pull between them notched up another level. It was only two days since she'd spoken to him on the phone, four days since she'd seen him. They'd parted in a wash of angry emotion, but she felt as hungry for him as if he'd been away in a war zone for a year.

"You were right all along," he said. "You *are* a girl."

She gave him a tight, wobbly smile. "Feel like reminding myself of the fact occasionally. This turned out to be one of those times."

What was a woman supposed to call it? Empowerment? So far it wasn't working as intended.

"I like those times." He let his roving gaze take in the shadowy V of the little cleavage on show. To Carmen her hormone-laced breasts already felt fuller than they had been a couple of weeks ago, but if Jack noticed, he didn't comment. His eyes had dropped to her high, spiky heels, then lifted to the usual flash and dangle of her earrings, the piled hair, the makeup put on by Kate with a slightly too-generous hand.

"Maybe I shouldn't have," Carmen said, speaking her doubt aloud.

"Are you kidding?"

"Maybe it sends the wrong message."

"Every damned inch of you is sending the wrong message, Carmen." He stepped close, daring her to resist touching him when he was just inches away—his mouth, his chest, that smoky look in his eyes. "Every inch of you sends the wrong message to me, even when you're wearing dirty denim shorts stuck all over with sawdust, and paint-stained shoes, and no makeup, and a twist tie from a bread bag to keep your hair back."

"I only did that once when my hair elastic broke." Her voice came out breathy, and he heard it.

"You're missing my point, sweetheart." His mouth was only an inch from hers now.

"Don't," she said.

"Why not, when I want to so bad." He reached for her, brushed her jawline with the tips of his fingers, let his mint-freshened breath wash over the sensitive skin below her ear. "And when you want to just as much. I know you do."

"Because this isn't why we're seeing each other tonight."

"You want it to be why."

"No."

"No?"

She closed her eyes, trying to gather the strength she needed to stay firm and push him away. It didn't come. Instead, she felt the brush of his mouth against her neck and the whisper of his fingers across her bare collarbone. She stood there. Was she swaying? The ground seemed unsteady beneath her feet. The whole universe tilted and changed when she was with this man.

"Carmen…" He began to kiss her more deeply, on the corner of her mouth, full on her lips.

She felt the dart of his tongue and then the sweet nip of his teeth drawing on her lower lip, coaxing her to open to him. She couldn't move. A moan of helpless need escaped her and he heard it as his own victory. His arms came around her and he was so warm and hard and strong and delicious, she was shaking when she held him, and she couldn't let him go.

"Are Cormack and Kate home?" he asked softly.

"Yes."

"Do you want to go in anyhow?"

"No. We need to talk first. Not *first*. We need to talk. We're not— Don't do this, Jack."

"Seems to me that you're doing it, too, sweetheart."

"I'm trying not to. I don't want to." While he stroked his hands down her back, and kept up a constant rain of those sweet, cajoling, hungry kisses.

"Why?"

"Because this isn't enough," she said. "This doesn't make up —it can't make up—for the places that are all wrong."

"It can! We have to work on it, not let it go."

"I can't. I don't know how."

"So you're throwing everything away."

"I don't see a choice."

"There's always a choice. When it's this strong, Carmen, you just have to take it on faith and—"

"No. No. Stop." Shakily she pushed him away and walked out of the house toward his car, parked in the street.

"You still want to eat?" He followed her, sounding angry and at sea. "What's the point?"

"I'm hungry," she snapped at him, because it was either *I'm hungry* or *I'm pregnant,* and she didn't want to give him her news that way.

Hungry and getting queasy from the emptiness in her stomach, and if she didn't find the right way to tell him about the baby tonight, it would only get harder. Everything would get harder.

They barely spoke on the way to the restaurant—a steakhouse not far away. It was one of Cormack's favorites, and served fabulous food but it wasn't in a great neighborhood. She asked Jack about his weekend with Ryan, and he was almost evasive on the subject. "Ask me again tomorrow. I have a few things to think about first."

They reached the restaurant and she wondered if she should just break her news to him in the car before they went in. Or wait until he'd had a beer? Wait until dessert? She began to frame some words, but they stuck in her throat. How did you say something this momentous when you had no idea of what you wanted or how the father of your baby would react? When you loved him but had to push him away?

With every passing minute she grew less certain. Jack's effect on her senses made her dizzy, flooded her with the beguiling, untrustworthy idea that their chemical connection was all that mattered, as he'd claimed.

It wasn't.

She had to be stronger than this.

Something was going on in the far corner of the sprawling restaurant parking lot as they walked toward the entrance from his car. Carmen saw a police patrol car parked at the curb and two young uniformed officers engaging with a man dressed in a baggy coat and shapeless hat. A streetlight shone on a litter of broken glass scattered across the oil-stained ground.

"Hang on, what's this?" Jack muttered, his attention immediately caught. "I know those guys. We went through a training course together."

He altered direction at once, turning away from the brightly lit restaurant entrance and heading toward the edge of the lot where the altercation had grown louder and more confused. Carmen grabbed his arm and stopped him. "There's no need for you to step in, Jack."

He turned and looked at her. "I'm not stepping in, I'm making sure they don't need a third pair of hands."

"They don't. You're back in uniform tomorrow, not today. This is not your job tonight."

"They're pretty inexperienced. I'm a lot more senior."

"They have the situation under control. Can we please just go eat?" Carmen heard her own voice sounding too hard and tight and hostile, while what she really felt was fear. She saw something that she couldn't control—Jack's actions and her own emotion—coming at her like a speeding train, and she was tied to the track, the track of her own reaction, helpless to move.

He froze where he stood and looked at her closely, reading her with his street instinct for trouble. "Is this the same argument we've had twice before? The whole unnecessary-risk-taking thing?"

"Of course it is! You're stepping into a situation you don't need to be in, you've sniffed out yet another opportunity to show off or play the hero. I don't know which. But you're taking a risk you don't need to take, while I'm telling you not to." Her voice cracked. "And you're ignoring me."

*The way Dad did, that rainy night. The way Dad always did, and Cormack and I lived on a knife-edge of fear for months, and Dad ignored us.*

Jack looked at her, mouth and eyes steady, body coiled tight. She couldn't read his eyes, but his words were clear enough. "You're wrong, Carmen. This time you're wrong. This time I'm not the one who needs to change."

"I'm scared," she whispered, and so help her, she was—panicky and terrified and sick in a way she didn't have words for, even though it was all too familiar. Dad, then Kate and now Jack.

"Then your fear is the problem that needs to be dealt with," he told her gently. "Not my actions." He squeezed her shoulders and turned back to study the actions of his fellow officers, ignoring the desperate way she pulled on his arm.

"Please, Jack, look, the guy has his hands in the air. He's showing he doesn't have a weapon. They're sending him on his way. They're going back to their vehicle. It's over. Let's go eat."

But Jack was motionless, deaf to her pleading, and hadn't taken his eyes from the man.

"Wait…" he muttered. "What's he got in his coat? I have a bad feeling about this."

He took no notice of Carmen's drag on his arm, still had his gaze fixed intently on the man in the shabby coat. He took some steps forward, with Carmen still clinging to him and only just fighting her fear enough to breathe.

The patrol car pulled out from the curb and sped up along the street. The man began to walk crookedly toward a tiny side alley that led in the direction of some shapeless gray buildings backing a nearby rail line. The guy stopped for a moment and looked down into the gaped opening at the bulky front of his coat, where there must be a button missing. He muttered some garbled words.

With the fear still pounding in her ears, stuffing them with the sound of her own rapid heartbeat, Carmen thought she heard a stray cat miaowing somewhere.

"Wait!" Jack muttered again, his low tone urgent this time.

Without warning, he shook himself free of her locked arms and broke into a low, loping run, saying something in a voice too deep and indistinct for Carmen to hear. The guy in the coat had almost disappeared into the dark of the alley. There was *no reason* for Jack to be doing this! Why did he have to go after the guy, when he was harmless and already retreating from the scene?

Carmen opened her mouth to speak, but no words would come.

*I won't be here when you get back.*

The threat dammed back inside her. It didn't matter that she hadn't said it. She *couldn't* say it. But Jack would get the message, a few minutes from now, when he showed up at the restaurant and found her gone. He'd disappeared down the alley. Hadn't even looked back at her, as if he'd forgotten she was even here. She had no idea why he was pursuing this. Did he think he was going to make a drug bust that his fellow officers had missed? Did one missed drug bust matter?

She walked the short distance to the main street, where the steady river of traffic suggested that a cab should come past soon. If none did, she'd go into the restaurant and call for one. Anger slowly began to squeeze aside her fear. Jack Davey was the father of her baby, although he didn't know it yet, and for the third and most critical time in their relationship, he'd ignored her pleas and her needs and chosen to play the hero instead.

What had he seen just now, inside this guy's coat? What had he heard? It had sounded like Tux when he meowed, but it wasn't a cat.

The two officers were long gone, and Jack had no illusions about how Carmen would take this—she wouldn't still be at the restaurant when he got back—but he had no choice. He wasn't going to risk letting this guy out of his sight. He hadn't even dared to turn and give Carmen a last look in case he missed some crucial detail. Every hair on his body had stood to attention, just now, and his cop's intuition must be clogging the airwaves with its powerful signals.

He would swear that the man with the dirt-encrusted hair and unlaced shoes weaving erratically down the back alley ahead of him had a living, breathing baby held against his chest.

The guy hadn't yet realized that Jack was following him. Completely unarmed…out of practice at this. To be honest, he didn't want to make a move too soon. Not until he'd thought the situation through, learned a little more about what he was dealing with.

For a start, the man's gait said he was either drugged, drunk, mentally ill or all three at once. He let out garbled strings of words at intervals, stopped a couple of times during his progression along the alley and opened his coat, peered into it, made some kind of adjustment. Both times his gestures looked tender.

Okay, so he's protecting the baby, he's not intending harm, Jack concluded.

But that intention might not last. Paranoid thought processes could lead to irrational and violent outcomes. If Jack confronted the guy and he saw it as a threat to take the baby away…

No. No confrontations, he decided.

Where was the guy going?

Last time Jack had patrolled this neighborhood, there were a couple of illegal squats nearby, as well as some makeshift shelters beside the freight line. Did the guy live in one of these? Or in a seedy residential hotel Jack also remembered as being in the area?

He followed at a safe distance as the man turned out of the alley and into a deserted sidestreet. The guy passed beneath a streetlamp and Jack distinctly heard that meowing sound again.

*Carmen, would you still think I was just playing the hero if you could hear that sound and see the way this guy is moving?*

He closed the distance by ten yards or so, while the

man stopped beneath the lamp and checked on the tiny bundle in his coat once more.

It wasn't a cat. The streetlamp clearly showed the rounded shape of a baby's head, covered in one of those stretchy little hospital baby caps, which Jack remembered from when Ryan was a newborn.

Hell! Newborn?

Should the baby still be in a hospital somewhere? It might only be a few hours old. It looked small enough for that.

The guy started walking again. He must have the baby in a front carrier beneath that baggy, shabby coat, because much of the time he kept his hands free. He'd raised both of them in the air when the two officers had wanted to see a weapon. No sign of violence or resistance. Still. They should have patted him down, despite their inexperience. They should have noticed the bulge in front, even though it was small.

Meanwhile, the guy still hadn't seen Jack or shown any uneasiness about his surroundings.

Jack closed the distance a little more, to just twelve yards or so.

The man turned into another street, lined with run-down clapboard two-family houses with small yards and exterior stairs on one side, leading from ground level to the second dwelling on the upper floor. At the fourth house, the man left the sidewalk and headed down the side yard to one of those sets of wooden stairs.

He saw Jack, finally—Jack was a bare three yards

away, so he knew it was crunch time—and stopped with one foot poised on the first step.

"Everything okay, there, buddy?" Jack asked pleasantly.

"Got it now."

"Need some help?" He closed the distance to a couple of feet, almost encroaching on the other man's body space. The guy didn't smell good.

"Careful, man." He shielded the bundle with his arm.

"Just wondering if you need any help." Jack followed him up the first couple of stairs. "Look like you have your hands full, there. Is somebody waiting for you upstairs?"

"I can handle everything." The man retreated two more steps up, and again Jack followed, moving slow and casual.

"Well, you know, I've changed a few diapers in my time," he said. "My boy's nearly ten years old, but I still remember. Can be tough, taking care of a baby."

"I got it in hand. I got it okay."

"Still, you know, I thought maybe you were having some trouble back there in the parking lot."

*Where's Carmen now?*

The thought slashed across his concentration as he pictured the parking lot, remembered her tightly wound body. He had to fight to focus on the man in front of him.

"Wasn't having no trouble," the guy said. "I'm doing great. Got my baby boy, fresh home from the hospital this morning, and nobody's going to take him away. Making sure of that. See?" He smiled with sly triumph and cunning. "See the insurance I got?"

He reached into the back of the pouch-like carrier where the baby nestled, and Jack's stomach clenched when he saw a flash of metal. There was a small but lethal-looking knife in the man's hand, and the baby-blue stretch cap rested softly against the edge of the blade.

## Chapter Twelve

"You are home way too soon!" Kate accused Carmen at the front door. She peered past her older sister. "And you came by cab! I'm gonna kill the guy!"

"He's just an innocent taxi driver, Kate," Carmen joked wearily.

"So tell me what he said! And you know I'm talking about Jack Davey, not the cab driver."

"I didn't even get a chance to tell him."

"How come?" She drew Carmen inside.

"Oh, this shining suit of armor dropped out of the sky and he of course had to climb right into it and jump on a big white horse and go chase someone. Where's Cormack?"

"Out. While I get you something to eat and drink, you have to talk to me. Seriously. Come sit in the kitchen."

"Seriously, I had a panic attack."

"You don't have panic attacks."

"I've had three since Jack and I have been seeing each other. All sourced in the same problem. He does things... takes these risks...tells me he's fine...reminds me of Dad *so much.*" She stifled a sob, ambushed by the depth of her emotion. "I told him last week that I couldn't do this anymore, couldn't tie my life to his when he does this to me, but then I had to see him tonight and it happened again. It just keeps happening, Katie, and I can't deal with it."

"What happened? Tell me the whole story, Carmie."

"I was clinging to his arm. There was this guy."

"Where? When?"

"As we were walking across the parking lot to the restaurant."

"And the guy was...?"

"I'm not sure. Drugged, maybe. Two cops had already checked him out and let him go, but that wasn't good enough for Jack. I couldn't breathe. He told me it was my problem. He left me standing there and disappeared down an alley, and if he's arrived back at the restaurant and found me gone— Well, has he called?"

"No, Carmie."

"This is really over now. It's over."

"Don't you still want to tell him about the baby?"

"I'll e-mail," she snapped at her sister.

"Carmen, that's not an answer."

"I know."

* * *

"Easy. Easy, now," Jack said to the guy, keeping his peripheral vision on the glint of the knife. "Is this your place?"

"I got it set up for him." He looked proud, but his eyes were glazed and unsteady. They darted around, half-fearful, half-belligerent, in search of imaginary enemies.

Jack had already crossed "drunk" off his list of possibilities. There could still be some drugs involved. Unfortunately, they weren't the ones the guy needed. He was clearly mentally ill and off his meds.

"So let's take him inside and get him settled," Jack suggested calmly. "You said he's only just home from the hospital. When was he born?"

"Three days ago. He had a breathing problem, so they wouldn't let him home as soon as usual. That wasn't my fault."

"Of course it wasn't."

"He went home this morning."

"But home wasn't here, this morning."

"Home is here now." The blade pressed against the stretchy blue knit fabric again.

"Easy with that thing, buddy, you don't want to hurt him."

"He's got the hat. I won't hurt him." He added darkly, "Unless I have to."

Jack's scalp tightened and prickled. He didn't doubt that the guy meant what he said. "Let's take him inside."

They went up the rickety stairs. Jack waited for the guy to challenge his presence, but he had his mind fixed on the homecoming for his baby and barely seemed to notice when Jack entered the pitiful dwelling right behind him, still trying to project unthreatening helpful friendliness in every line of his body and every word he said.

What was Carmen doing at this moment? She must surely be home by now. Angry. Upset. No clue where he was. He thought of the cell phone in his pocket and wanted desperately to call her but didn't dare. He might only get one chance at a call, and that had to be a request for backup and a hostage-negotiation team.

There was a mattress on the living-room floor, and a mess of cheap furnishings and scattered clothing in the two bedrooms Jack glimpsed down a short, narrow corridor. The kitchen was cluttered and filthy, apart from one clean, new dish towel spread on a piece of bench. The cloth was set with a neat row of new and gleaming plastic baby bottles that were dotted with colorful boy baby motifs—trains and trucks and balls.

Beside the mattress in the other room there was a cardboard box that looked like a pet bed, lined with some pieces of folded blanket and a flannel sheet. There was also a stack of ill-assorted disposable diapers of all different brands, sizes and styles. They looked as if they'd been stolen from diaper bags and strollers at random. Several cans of infant formula were similarly mismatched.

"I have everything in place," the man said. "No one's gonna say I'm not taking care of him right. He's my baby, too."

"What's his name, buddy?" Jack asked.

"She's calling him Troy."

"She's his mom?"

"Not anymore. I have him now."

"Are you calling him Troy?"

"Helen of Troy. I'm calling him Homer."

"Homer was the Greek guy who wrote about Helen of Troy."

"Can't call a boy baby Helen."

"No, I guess you can't. And how about you? What's your name?"

"Steve. Sometimes it's Bartok."

"Steve. I'm Jack." He looked around and infused his voice with approval. "You sure do have this place fixed up nice for a baby."

"I got the bottles and everything," the guy said proudly. His face darkened. "And I got the knife for if she comes for him."

Kate made Carmen a grilled ham and cheese sandwich and a mug of canned French onion soup and coaxed her to eat the offerings as if she was a fussy two-year-old. "Hey, finish the soup. You're eating for two, remember?"

Secretly warmed and nourished by the unfamiliar role reversal, Carmen obediently sipped on a second mug of soup, while her heart sat right beside the silent phone, bleeding. She'd changed into black sweatpants and a gray T-shirt because the slinky red dress wasn't needed anymore, and hadn't helped in the first place.

"I can't believe he hasn't called you!" Kate said.

This didn't help, and maybe Katie could tell, because

she pressed her lips together, took in Carmen's silence and didn't say another word about Jack.

"What're you doing here, anyhow?" Steve said, after they'd been talking for probably twenty minutes, maybe longer. "What're you doing in my place? Who are you?"

Jack had lost his sense of time passing and didn't want to look at his watch in case this gave Steve unwanted reminders of the outside world and fed a paranoia that was, so far, thank heaven, pretty benign.

"Just trying to be helpful," he said. "I'm a dad, I remember how it feels to have a new baby home from the hospital." He was still trying to get a feel for the situation, get the man's trust. "I'll head out of here once you have him settled."

The baby had begun to cry, which helped Jack's case. Steve looked as if the crying would fray his edgy nerves pretty fast. He changed the little boy's diaper. Jack stood by with a box of baby wipes but Steve acted possessive with the child, using his broad back, still clad in the coat, to shield his actions from Jack's vision.

The baby kept crying, and Steve seemed clumsy with the diaper, the stretchy baby suit and the wipes. The process took a long time. From what Jack could see, the tiny boy looked healthy and normal, and his cry was strong. He wasn't in any immediate danger, but his mother must be distraught.

"He needs his bottle," Steve muttered, when he

finally had the clean diaper in place and the snaps on the baby's clothing done up. "I gotta heat it up."

"How about I do that for you while you soothe him? Rock him in your arms. They like that."

"I gotta take care of him. Has to be me. She won't let me anywhere near him. She thinks I've gone wrong again."

"But you have him now, so you can accept a little help. Just for this first evening at home. You can let me heat up the bottle just this once. After that, you'll do fine."

When had he gone off his meds, Jack wondered. He'd made a rough-and-ready cop's diagnosis, the way he'd been trained. He was going to treat this as schizophrenia, even if the guy's doctors might have a more detailed or slightly different analysis. He knew a bit about schizophrenics.

How bad did Steve get when his delusions took hold? Did he have any other weapons stashed around the apartment? Did he have roommates? Where were they, and what kind of a condition were they in? Might they show up without warning and shatter the fragile balance and trust he was trying to achieve?

He took one of the cans of ready-mixed formula Steve had stacked up beside the wall and eased his way toward the kitchen, ready to concede the issue for the time being if the guy showed any more inclination to object.

But he didn't, he just nodded, wincing at the high-pitched sounds of his newborn so close to his ear. "Gotta get him something to eat. Then I have to call her up and tell her how it's going to be with me and Homer, and me taking over as secretary of the U.N. and Head of U.S. Defense."

"Okay, so we'll feed the baby first," Jack said, still calm and casual.

In the kitchen he couldn't find a kettle, and there was no microwave. There was a dirty cooking pot in the sink, however, so he scrubbed as best he could with an ancient scourer, then rinsed it out and filled it with water, wondering if the stove would even work. It was electric, old and battered like the one Carmen and her brother had wrestled out of his own kitchen two months ago.

*Stop thinking about her…*

He held his hand over the first hotplate he tried, but there was no change in temperature. He tried another and felt a rush of relief when he got some heat. He poured the ready-mixed formula into a bottle and stood it in the pot of water. This was going to take a while, but he hadn't wanted to pour the formula directly into a cooking pot that still wasn't all that clean. He checked on Steve and the baby—one rocking, the other crying. Good so far.

But then he saw that Steve had the knife pressed against the baby's head again.

"You gotta stop crying, Homer," he crooned. "Is she making you do this? Is she getting you to cry like this to stress me out? She's sending the messages into your head, isn't she?"

Jack knew it wouldn't take much for the situation to go very, very bad.

He slid his cell phone from his pocket, flipped it

open, pressed a couple of buttons, then spoke softly to one of his colleagues on the force—no time for social niceties such as establishing whether he knew the guy who'd picked up the phone.

"This is Officer Jack Davey," he said quietly. "I'm at 615 Railroad Avenue, Fairmount Park, and I have a potential hostage situation, involving a newborn child…"

Turning his back on Steve to mask the call had been a mistake. He felt the point of the man's knife prick into his hand, and then the cell phone was gone.

Thrown to the floor.

Crushed under Steve's foot.

Kicked beneath the stove.

"You don't wanna use those things," Steve said helpfully. "They drain off your thoughts and send them to people you don't want. I got my land line, but we don't wanna make no calls unless we have to. Could scare the baby."

Still Jack hadn't called.

Carmen felt tired and old. She took a shower, urged into it by Kate, then they sat in front of TV while Kate flipped through the channels on the remote. News, movies, reruns, cartoons. "Can you stop on one thing for, oh, a whole ten seconds, please, Katie? You're giving me motion sickness."

Or rather, morning sickness. At nine in the evening.

"Sorry," Kate said.

She stopped on a local news channel, and they caught two items of international news, some presidential politics, and then the announcement of a breaking local story. Something about a mentally ill man, a hostage negotiation team, a baby and a knife. Carmen let it wash over her almost without hearing, until Kate suddenly sat up straighter. "Carmen! Oh, shoot, Carmen, are you listening to this?"

Seconds later she heard the reporter say Jack's name.

The early June night would have been mild, but a breeze had sprung up, and it cut through Carmen's sweatpants and T-shirt as she stood in the dingy street. It was eleven o'clock. Kate pressed a jacket into her hands and she nodded and put it on, then said to her baby sister, "Go home, Katie, you don't need to be here, and you have a breakfast shift in the morning."

"Like I'm going to leave you here on your own."

"I'm not on my own."

"Cops? News reporters? Those scary SWAT guys? And the baby's poor mom? I'm your sister!" She hugged Carmen fiercely.

Was this what it took to get Kate to grow up and discover her loving and generous side?

It wasn't worth it.

Not for a second.

Right now Carmen would happily trade Kate staying a teenage brat forever, if it meant that Jack would come out of that dingy-looking clapboard house in the next three seconds, alive and safe.

And the baby.

The baby had to be alive and safe, too.

The mother was distraught, sobbing and wrapped in a blanket, in the care of a female police officer who was successfully keeping the media at bay. "He's off his meds," she moaned. "He could do anything. And when he's delusional he gets so strong and so fast. Please don't let the officer try to take him down. No force. Please. My baby…my baby."

"Jack must have known," Carmen muttered, half to Kate and half to herself. "He must have seen the baby with that guy, after the other cops left. That's why he followed him, and he didn't have a chance to explain."

"You love him, don't you?" Kate said. "You really… just…*love* him."

"Yes." Because it was that simple.

"You're going to deal with the risk taking. You're going to take that risk yourself?"

"If he'll let me."

*If he comes out of that building safe.*

"I don't think I have a choice." The familiar fear welled up inside her, but something was different this time. Something was missing. What was it?

"Is anything happening?" she heard Kate mutter. "Sheesh, how long is this going to take?" She peered down the street. They'd been kept here at the end of it by police barriers. The street itself was closed to traffic, but there were two or three TV news crews stationed as close as they were permitted to get. "I thought they had experts in place," Kate finished.

They did—the hostage negotiator, the SWAT team— but that didn't mean the standoff would be resolved quickly. Nor did it guarantee that Jack or the baby would be okay.

Carmen's heart jumped into her throat again and she felt sick to her stomach. But still there was something missing that she couldn't name.

She did some jittery soul searching and finally came up with the answer.

In the midst of all this—her nauseating fear, her skittering pulses, her need to cling to Kate, her aching love for Jack and her empathy for the distraught mother nearby—there was one emotion she didn't feel.

Anger.

She wasn't angry with him.

She understood why he'd gone after that man tonight, and she no longer blamed him for it. She trusted him, trusted his instincts and his priorities and his inner strength, the way she'd never trusted her dad's. The feeling of standing on crumbling ice waiting for it to give way—the feeling that she and Cormack had experienced over and over during the endless year of her dad's decline—was gone.

Jack wouldn't let the ice give way.

He just wouldn't.

He'd find a way to hold it up or he'd die trying.

Which meant that even if the worst happened, Carmen would be left with the things she really needed—the good things, the memories, the respect, the trust… All the things she hadn't been left with when her father died, all the things his weakness had robbed her of.

And the worst wouldn't happen. Not this time. She

believed this and pinned herself to it with every hope in her heart.

"Katie, this could take all night or longer," she told her sister gently.

"How can you stand it? How can you sound so calm?"

"I'm not calm. A little calmer. I've…worked out a couple of things."

"Are you going to wait?"

"Just try dragging me away."

"The police negotiator hasn't even got the guy to start talking yet."

"I'm going to wait."

"In that case, I'm waiting with you."

Roughly twenty minutes later, a woman's voice spoke through the fog of Carmen's emotion and fierce, impatient hope. Carmen hadn't even noticed her approach. "Carmen? You're here, too?"

She turned to find Terri Kruger standing there in jeans, a suede jacket and a pair of expensive camel-colored boots. "We saw it on the news," she said numbly to Jack's ex-wife.

"Same here. Jay did. I…I don't know why I had to come. Yes, I do. I mean, of course I do. He's Ryan's father. This is—" she laughed "—unreal."

"I know."

"He's such a good person. A good man. The world needs heroes, even if I, personally, did not want to live with one."

"Is that what made you leave, Terri? Really? Because you didn't want to live with a hero?"

The other woman shrugged inside her designer jacket. After a moment she admitted, "No. Not really."

"Then why?"

"He refused to go after the things I wanted, that's all."

"What things did you want."

"Success. Just success."

"There's more than one kind of success."

Terri's face hardened a little. Her jaw squared and her eyes flashed. "I wanted the kind you can measure. The kind that people can see the moment they look at you. At your house, your car and your kid's activities and clothes. Those things are important to me. I'm not going to apologize for that. I have it now, everything I've ever wanted, and I'm very happy. Jack just wasn't interested. I got so angry with him. And I still am. I hear myself saying things to him, still, even now, three years after we first separated, that I wouldn't say to anyone else in the world." She looked at Carmen. "You think I'm a total bitch, but I'm not. I'm just very, very different from Jack."

"You were wrong for each other. Is that what you're saying?"

"We were wrong for each other. And I couldn't deal with it. I lashed out." She looked around her—down the blocked-off street and at the police and TV crews. "I still can't deal with it. Are you going to stay here all night?"

"If I have to."

"Well, I'm not."

"Does Ryan know that this is happening?"

"No, thank goodness. And I won't let him find out

unless there's no choice. I'll give Jack an hour, then if he hasn't come out of there, I'll go home and get some rest in my own bed. I have Ryan and Jay and my unborn baby to think of." She gave a faint smile.

"You're pregnant?"

"Yes." She rested her hand against her lower stomach.

"Congratulations, Terri."

*Me, too.*

As far as Carmen was concerned, it was for her unborn baby's sake that she'd stay here as long as it took.

## Chapter Thirteen

"I'm not talking to no federal agent," Steve said.

"So talk to me."

"You should leave."

"Let me stay and help you with this. Is there anything you want to say to anyone?"

"I can't hear, they're all yelling too loud."

"Who's yelling, Steve?"

"It's Bartok. My name's Bartok."

"Who's yelling, Bartok?"

"The U.N. delegates. They're having a session of the Security Council on how they're going to kill Homer."

He sat on the mattress with the baby in his arms and the knife in his hand. He hadn't let the little newborn bundle out of his touch for a second, and every scenario

Jack came up with for disarming him and snatching the baby ended in too great a risk that the tiny boy would bear the brunt. It was a risk he wasn't prepared to take. He knew the baby's mother was waiting outside.

He kept getting flashbacks to three months ago, the night he and his partner, Russ, had shot that woman, the night he'd been shot himself.

*It's not going to happen this time. There's no blood getting spilled tonight. This one's going to work out in the end, with no one getting hurt.*

The determination rang in his head like a vow, and he thought of Carmen again—hell, he thought of Carmen every minute. He needed to walk out of here in triumph for her sake, for the sake of her past loss, her anger about her dad, her faith in the future.

He was going to walk out of here with a whole and healthy baby in his arms for Carmen.

"They don't want him and me taking over as Secretary of Defense, you see," Steve said.

Jack dragged his focus back to the man, the baby and the knife. "So how about we get some sleep and deal with this in the morning," he suggested.

"Not safe to sleep."

"Homer's sleeping. That bottle really filled him up nice. He got such a contented baby look on his face. You must be pretty tired, too."

"He's not really a baby."

"No?"

"He's carrying a presence in his soul."

"Well, it looks like a pretty sleepy, contented presence right now. He's a beautiful little guy. Why don't you take a nap right beside him, there, and I'll keep checking that he's okay."

"Don't need to sleep."

*But I need you to...*

Jack checked his watch without letting Steve see. Two-seventeen in the morning. He hid a yawn, and fought the aching plea in his body. He must not sleep. He must get Steve to sleep. And he must not think about Carmen, all sweet and warm in her bed, not knowing that this was happening, hating him.

The police negotiator and the SWAT team would still be in position at the end of the street, and some of those guys had probably been wanting to blast their way in here for the past three hours, but Jack had managed to get through to them that the risk was too great.

The moment Steve got agitated and his paranoid delusions built stronger, he moved the knife half an inch and into position—not against the little knit cap anymore, but directly in contact with the baby's fragile throat. His movements were less careful and gentle than they'd been at first. When the baby was crying, earlier, Jack had thought he'd seen some drops of blood. It would take a split second to end this standoff in the worst possible way.

*I have to outlast him. I have to let* him *get tired. I cannot risk the baby getting hurt.*

For the baby's own sake. For the baby's mom. For Steve, once he was back on his meds and could understand what he'd done.

And for Carmen.

He willed himself to grow more alert, and just kept talking in as quiet and unthreatening a way as he could, while he watched and waited.

Dawn would soon break.

From her position seated on a low, gritty piece of concrete wall, Carmen saw the first signs of morning light in the eastern sky and gave a convulsive shiver. Her hair and shoulders were drenched in dew. True to Terri's intention, she had gone home hours ago. And Kate had retreated to the car to sleep, even though she still refused to actually leave.

Two hours ago Jack had communicated to the police negotiator that he wanted to handle this on his own. No more attempts to talk to Steve on the phone, please, no action from the SWAT team.

Since then…nothing.

The baby's mother sat huddled in the back of a police van, too drained even to cry. Only one of the TV news crews remained. The others had gone to sniff out more-promising and dramatic stories elsewhere. Someone said there was a factory fire in Elizabeth—dramatic footage, while nothing was happening here.

Nothing except the rhythm of quiet, regular foot-steps coming down the blocked-off street.

Oh, dear Lord, it was Jack, and he had a baby-blue bundle cradled in his arms.

Carmen didn't believe what she was seeing at first. He walked slowly and calmly, and if she'd had any doubt about what might have happened in there, the quiet smile on his face told her that everything was all right. He looked weary and a little creaky in the joints after the long night, but solid as a rock.

The baby's mother jumped to her feet, moaning and crying. Carmen was crying, too, jerky sobs of relief that shook her shoulders even though she barely felt them as she uncurled her stiff, tired body from its uncomfortable position on the wall. Jack hadn't seen her yet, and in the midst of her relief she felt scared, because she had no idea how he'd react to her presence, after the way they'd parted last night.

A plain-clothes police officer went up to Jack to get a debrief, and Jack told him, "No dramas. Send the paramedics in. The guy's asleep, but he's twitchy. He's going to need sedation and to get back on his meds as soon as possible. The baby's fine. Unharmed and fed and well."

"Oh, oh, oh!" the mother said, and Jack passed the little bundle across to her. "Oh, baby. Oh, Troy, sweetheart. Oh, thank you, God!" She cradled the baby against her breast, kissing him, crying over him, the joy and relief making her glow and tremble.

"Steve had bottles and diapers and formula, ma'am," Jack told her. "He did pretty well."

"He's delusional, I thought he'd hurt him," the mother said. "He's…he's capable of it when he's like this. I was so, so scared."

"He had a knife." Jack gave this to the plain-clothes officer as he spoke. It would go into a sealed bag as evidence. There would have to be a hearing on the man's psychiatric state. "But we didn't get to that point."

He saw Carmen at that moment, and she knew he was shocked that she was here. He hadn't expected it. The fact was written in every line of his body, and etched deep into the changed expression on his face. He wasn't smiling anymore.

If only her body would move!

Willing the cold and stiffness away, she stumbled toward him at last. "Oh, Jack."

"Hell, Carmen, what are you doing here? Oh, Lord…"

"Waiting for you."

"All night, sweetheart?" His arms came around her, and the sweet, warm heat of belonging flooded through her.

"I came as soon as I saw it on the news. And Katie's asleep in the car."

"I thought you probably didn't even know what had happened. I didn't know if this had made it onto the news in time. I thought you'd be home in bed and I so much wanted to be there with you, lying in your arms. But I saw the baby, Carmen, and when I found out he was newborn…"

"I'm not blaming you. I'm not angry with you."

"You were. You were shaking with anger, outside the restaurant. Anger and fear."

"And you told me it was my problem, and you were right. Oh, Jack—"

He kissed the top of her head, tightening his arms around her. "Let's find someplace we can really talk, sweetheart."

"Jack…?" It was one of his fellow cops, no doubt

wanting more detail on the events of the night. There'd be statements, reports, charges, evaluations.

"Can it wait?" Jack said.

"My thoughts exactly," the man replied. "I wanted to suggest you go home and get some rest. Give us a call when you're ready to come in and file a report. Technically, you were acting as a private citizen when you followed the guy home."

"Yeah, but my doctor says I'm the hero type." Jack gave an upside-down grin.

"Even heroes get time off. Go, Jack. Looks like you have a few things to sort out." He gave Carmen a curious, smiling glance and she blushed.

"Something like that," Jack told him.

"We should go wake up Kate," Carmen said.

"She can drop us back at the restaurant before she heads home in your car."

"Are they open for breakfast?"

"Don't you remember? My car's still there."

"Oh, of course, you're right…" It seemed like half a lifetime ago that he'd picked her up and driven to the steakhouse.

They shook Kate gently awake. She took in Jack's presence and scrambled out of the vehicle so she could fling her arms around him and plant a lip-smacking kiss on his cheek. "You're safe. And so is the baby. I can tell just from Carmen's face."

Jack sketched out what had happened during the long night, and Kate hugged him again. "Do I get to be proud of you?" she asked almost shyly.

"Hope so," he said, sounding gruff. There was a lot still to resolve, and a lot to talk about, and all three of them knew what Kate was asking—was Jack going to stay in Carmen's life? And for how long?

To that, Carmen had no answers yet.

"We're going to pick up his car from the restaurant parking lot," she said. "Do you want to drop us there, then drive mine home?"

Fully aware of the pull of questions and unfinished business between the two of them, Kate nodded. "Sure, I can drive." She held out her hand for the keys and delivered Carmen and Jack to his car a couple of minutes later. "Have a good time, okay?" She touched Carmen's shoulder then kissed her quickly on the cheek. "Talk, you two!" she ordered.

The sun had peeked above the horizon of urban buildings to the east, and the air already felt much warmer. Morning traffic had begun to build. Kate turned out of the parking lot and drove away, and Carmen and Jack were alone. It was too early in the morning for the restaurant's breakfast shift to have arrived.

"Where do you want to go?" Jack asked.

"Anywhere, as long as it's with you. Am I allowed to say that? Let me say it, Jack, even if it doesn't fit with anything I said last night."

He hugged her hard, muttering words that she couldn't understand as he pressed his lips to the top of her head. "What's changed, Carmen?"

"I have," she said. "I'm not sure how. Maybe because what's just happened was so stark and clear-cut. Maybe because it involved a tiny baby and a distraught mother. I can separate the strands in my feelings now."

"You had to have been scared. It killed me that I couldn't talk to you. He broke my cell phone and kicked it under the stove. I didn't know you were waiting here, but even if I had I wouldn't have dared to get the negotiator to put you on the line because Steve was hanging by a thread, he could have thought you were a threat. You must have been terrified."

"Of course I was. But I wasn't angry. That was the difference."

"You were angry when I went to follow him."

"Because I didn't know what you'd seen. I've had the whole night to think about this, Jack, and it's different. You're different. You're not my dad. When Dad used to scare me, driving when he was almost too drunk to stand, driving in the snow or the pouring rain, driving the younger kids around so he was risking their lives, too, the anger in me got so mixed up with the fear. Those emotions fed off each other and made each other stronger. Just worse. In every way. Last night it was different. When I found out there was a baby involved, I knew you had to do what you did. How could you not have taken that risk, when a helpless human life was at stake? I understood that I'd been wrong to hold you back. I was still scared, but I could deal with it. Something about your courage and your certainty made me strong and certain, too. And I didn't keep getting all those destructive flashbacks to Dad. You're not him. Cormack tried to tell me so, just a few days ago, but I couldn't listen then."

"Cormack defended me?"

"He likes you."

"I can't imagine him having that kind of heart-to-heart with you. He's not exactly a guy who talks a lot."

"Oh, he didn't talk a lot. He just pointed out the ways you'd reacted when life hit you sideways. And he was right. When guys like Cormack do talk, they make sense."

"I've had some doubts, myself, about who I was, whether I was the man I needed to be. Terri's always stressed Jay's success with money and position, as if they're the only things that count. She acted as if I was so much of a failure that she felt sorry for me, and I almost began to believe she was right."

"No!"

"I go down when I'm kicked hard enough, the same as anyone."

"But then you get back up and fight, Jack Davey."

"Took me a while. I've been trying to prove myself to my son, trying to compete with Jay on Jay's terms, and on Wednesday after you left, I'd finally had enough."

"Enough of what?"

"Of seeing myself through her eyes. I investigated that bounced check and discovered it was just a glitch, not some major mismanagement of my finances, and that kind of set something straight in my thinking. I'm proud of who I am, proud of what I have and what I want and what I'm giving my son. Terri's never going to understand any of it, but that's her problem, not mine."

"I love you," Carmen blurted out.

"Yeah, same back at you." He grinned.

"You do?"

"So much, Carmen. And you know what?" His face glowed, then flared into another teasing grin. "I'm almost getting the impression Kate likes me, too."

"What are you working around to, here, Jack Davey?"

"A proposal, I think." The grin faded a little, and she caught the same uncertainty in his voice that she'd heard on the phone the first time he'd asked her out.

"Say that again?" she whispered. Like that first time, she was uncertain, too, and needed to make sure she'd really heard him right.

"Would you marry me, Carmen? Could you trust me that much?" His voice dropped still lower. "Do you love me that much? To share my life, even though we're not going to live in a palace. To deal with the risks, even when I can't give you guarantees. Every existence has risks. To love my son, because you love me. Do you want this?"

She started to cry, but she was laughing at the same time. "Yes, oh, yes!"

"Oh, Carmen... Hell, if you knew how scared I was that you wouldn't say that. Hey, don't cry..."

"Let me cry."

"Why, sweetheart?"

"You're asking me to marry you and I'm saying yes, and I haven't even told you about the baby yet."

"The—" his mouth dropped open *"—what?"*

"I'm pregnant, Jack. That's what I wanted to tell you last night over dinner, only we never had the chance."

"Oh, wow! Are you sure?"

"Kate made me take a test. She was the one who suspected that my churned-up stomach wasn't just happening because I was so emotional about you. And the test was positive."

"When's it due? A baby. Oh, wow!"

"I haven't had time to go to the doctor yet. But you know, there were a couple of times when we had a lot of trouble getting upstairs and grabbing one of those little packets from your bedside table drawer. I'm thinking late January or early Feb."

"Oh, wow."

"You keep saying that. Does it mean you're happy?"

He didn't answer directly, just shook his head with that bemused frown-slash-grin on his face. He was holding her, his hands splayed over her back, and she felt safe and wanted in his arms, and on tenterhooks at the same time. "Two baby siblings for Ryan," he said, "one before Christmas and one after."

"Yes, Terri let it slip last night."

"Last night?"

"She was here."

"I didn't see her."

"She said she'd give you an hour, and if you hadn't resolved the standoff by then, she was going home to bed. Me, I planned to stay as long as it took."

He kissed her. "You would have done that? Just stayed?"

"Days. Weeks."

"I just found out about Terri's pregnancy yesterday evening. She's known for a while. I'm…stunned. About our baby, not hers." He brushed a kiss across her mouth.

"Stunned and?"

"Daunted."

"And?"

"Happy, Carmen." He kissed her again. "Do you really doubt that?"

"No, I don't. How can I? I'm happy, too," she whispered. "I'm all three of those things, happy, daunted and stunned, and a whole lot more emotions we haven't even covered yet, and as long as we're going through them together, the happy part is all I care about."

"Hey, we were going to go somewhere quiet and nice, and here we still are in the restaurant parking lot."

"Have a feeling we might have been here longer than we think…"

The sun had risen fully, and it etched Jack's face with a warm morning glow. He looked weary and utterly gorgeous, strong and happy and king of his world, and there was something typical about their whole relationship that his proposal of marriage should take place now, like this, in a parking lot at dawn, and still seem totally right. Carmen laughed.

"What?" he whispered.

"This. You're fixing your house with your own hands. You first kissed me when we had a paint-stained rag in our hands. For our first date, to even get me to understand what you were asking, you had to push past Ryan making pony jumps in the house and my sister suffering a hangover in the background. Now the morning sun is turning you into king of the steakhouse parking lot, this would never happen in a movie, and it's perfect for who

I am and I love it. And with these kinds of precedents, I hate to think what our wedding day will be like, and where this baby of ours will decide to be born."

"Perfect day, perfect baby, wherever and whenever they happen, because we'll be together. That's all I know and all I care about."

"Me, too." She pressed her face against his roughened cheek and he kissed her with the promise of a lifetime in every touch of his mouth and his hands.

"Now, take me to bed," she whispered.

"You got it…" He picked her up effortlessly in his arms and turned toward the New Jersey sunrise, her knight and her hero. No armor, but still shining.

## *Epilogue*

They were married in September, and their baby was born on the fifth of February, after a sixteen-hour labor, which was, to be honest, quite a lot less fun than jack-hammering up a twelve-foot-by-eighteen-foot concrete bathroom floor.

Jack was there for every contraction, and the grin on his face when he took his new baby girl in his arms made every minute of the sixteen hours suddenly worthwhile.

Sarah Jane was beautiful.

Healthy and strong and beautiful.

"And a girl is great," Kate said when she came to the hospital to visit later that day, "because she'll be soooo much less trouble than a boy."

The really funny part was that she seemed perfectly sincere.

Holding Sarah Jane in her arms while Kate tentatively stroked her soft, pink baby cheek with one finger, Carmen looked over the top of Kate's head at Jack and they both smiled.

Yeah, Katie-girl, you've never given your sister a bad moment.

"How quickly they forget," Jack murmured.

Kate had started back at college after the New Year break, taking some classes to catch up on missed prerequisites before she would transfer to a more solid program in the coming fall. She had a new boyfriend, also aiming for a medical career, and the two of them were so competitive with each other that they seemed to cram for tests more often than they kissed.

"I never knew how hot a woman could get for a man's mind," Kate said.

The fact that six-foot-tall Ben had a body thoroughly buff from hours of practice with the college rowing team was completely irrelevant, of course.

"Don't listen to your aunt, Sarah Jane," Carmen told her baby daughter. "She's going to be a very bad influence, in as many different ways as she can possibly think of."

But she smiled as she said it, and Jack was smiling, too. This little girl had so many people who loved her, so many people to guide her on her path, so many directions to choose from as she grew.

She had a mother who'd gotten to this point by an unusual route, after half a lifetime of practice in the role, and she had the best daddy in the world.

\* \* \* \* \*

## Silhouette® Desire

**NEW YORK TIMES BESTSELLING AUTHOR**

# DIANA PALMER

A brand-new Long, Tall Texans novel

# IRON COWBOY

*Available March 2008*
*wherever you buy books.*

# "I have never felt more needed as a physician…"

—**Dr. Ricki Robinson,** real-life heroine

*Dr. Ricki Robinson is a Harlequin More Than Words award winner and an **Autism Speaks** volunteer.*

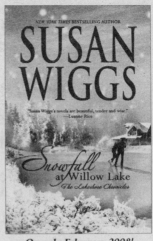

# HARLEQUIN Super Romance®

# *Bundles of Joy—*
## *coming next month to Superromance*

**Experience the romance, excitement and joy with 6 heartwarming titles.**

BABY, I'M YOURS #1476 by *Carrie Weaver*

ANOTHER MAN'S BABY
(The Tulanes of Tennessee)
#1477 by *Kay Stockham*

THE MARINE'S BABY (9 Months Later)
#1478 by *Rogenna Brewer*

BE MY BABIES (Twins)
#1479 by *Kathryn Shay*

THE DIAPER DIARIES (Suddenly a Parent)
#1480 by *Abby Gaines*

HAVING JUSTIN'S BABY (A Little Secret)
#1481 by *Pamela Bauer*

**Exciting, Emotional and Unexpected!**

*Look for these Superromance titles in March 2008.
Available wherever books are sold.*

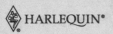

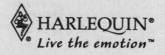

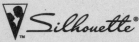

# COMING NEXT MONTH

SPECIAL EDITION

### #1885 THE SHEIK AND THE PREGNANT BRIDE—
**Susan Mallery**
*Desert Rogues*

When mechanic Maggie Collins was dispatched to Prince Qadir's desert home to restore his Rolls-Royce, she quickly discovered his love life could use a tune-up, too. Qadir was more than game, but would Maggie's pregnancy shocker stall the prince's engines?

### #1886 PAGING DR. DADDY—**Teresa Southwick**
*The Wilder Family*

Plastic surgeon to the stars David Wilder, back in Walnut River and the hospital his father once ran, was on a mission of mercy—to perform reconstructive surgery on a little girl badly injured in an auto accident. Would Courtney Albright, the child's resilient, irresistible mother, cause him to give up his L.A. ways for hometown love?

### #1887 MOMMY AND THE MILLIONAIRE—**Crystal Green**
*The Suds Club*

Unwed and pregnant, Naomi Shannon left her small town for suburban San Francisco, where she made fast friends at the local Laundromat. Sharing her ups and downs and watching the soaps with the Suds Club regulars was a relaxing treat…until gazillionaire David Chandler came along, and Naomi's life took a soap opera turn of its own!

### #1888 ROMANCING THE COWBOY—**Judy Duarte**
*The Texas Homecoming*

Someone was stealing from Granny, ranch owner Jared Clayton's adoptive mother. So naturally, he gave Granny's new bookkeeper, Sabrina Gonzalez, a real earful. But forget the missing money—a closer accounting of the situation showed that Jared had better watch out before Sabrina stole his heart!

### #1889 DAD IN DISGUISE—**Kate Little**
*Baby Daze*

When wealthy architect Jack Sawyer tried to cancel a sperm donation, he discovered his baby had already been born to single mother Rachel Reilly. So Jack went undercover as a handyman at her house to spy. Jack fell for the boy…and for Rachel—hard. But when the dad took off his disguise, all hell broke loose.…

### #1890 HIS MIRACLE BABY—**Karen Sandler**

To honor his deceased wife's wishes, sporting goods mogul Logan Rafferty needed a surrogate mother for their embryos. Her confidante Shani Jacoby would be perfect—but she was his sworn enemy. Still loyal to her best friend, though, Shani chose to carry Logan's miracle baby…and soon an even bigger miracle—of love—was on their horizon.

SSECNM0208